I have a body...

Bo grabbed her bag from the back seat and hopped out of the truck. Nora slid down from the pickup and followed him into the house.

The cabin was small but cozy, with an open floor plan and modern furnishings. Simple, yet sophisticated, the rustic-chic abode was a warm and welcoming retreat.

She took off her down parka, and when he did the same, she noticed the gun holstered on his hip. He took their coats and hung them on the hook near the door, along with his blazer, cowboy hat and sunglasses.

He looked at her, like he was gauging her reaction to his home.

To her new safe house.

Her heartbeat ratcheted up at having his full attention, which was more than a little overwhelming.

Forcing herself to relax, she stared back into his eyes. Deep brown and fathomless.

BIG SKY SAFE HOUSE

JUNO RUSHDAN

Harlequin
INTRIGUE

If you purchased this book without a cover you should be aware that this book is stolen property. It was reported as "unsold and destroyed" to the publisher, and neither the author nor the publisher has received any payment for this "stripped book."

MIX
Paper | Supporting responsible forestry
FSC® C021394

To all veterans. You are heroes.

Harlequin INTRIGUE™

ISBN-13: 978-1-335-69033-3

Big Sky Safe House

Copyright © 2025 by Juno Rushdan

All rights reserved. No part of this book may be used or reproduced in any manner whatsoever without written permission.

Without limiting the author's and publisher's exclusive rights, any unauthorized use of this publication to train generative artificial intelligence (AI) technologies is expressly prohibited.

This is a work of fiction. Names, characters, places and incidents are either the product of the author's imagination or are used fictitiously. Any resemblance to actual persons, living or dead, businesses, companies, events or locales is entirely coincidental.

For questions and comments about the quality of this book, please contact us at CustomerService@Harlequin.com.

TM and ® are trademarks of Harlequin Enterprises ULC.

Harlequin Enterprises ULC	HarperCollins Publishers
22 Adelaide St. West, 41st Floor	Macken House, 39/40 Mayor Street Upper,
Toronto, Ontario M5H 4E3, Canada	Dublin 1, D01 C9W8, Ireland
www.Harlequin.com	www.HarperCollins.com

Printed in Lithuania

Juno Rushdan is a veteran US Air Force intelligence officer and award-winning author. Her books are action-packed and fast-paced. Critics from *Kirkus Reviews* and *Library Journal* have called her work "heart-pounding James Bond–ian adventure" that "will captivate lovers of romantic thrillers." For a free book, visit her website: junorushdan.com.

Books by Juno Rushdan

Harlequin Intrigue

Ironside Protection Services

Big Sky Slayer
Big Sky Safe House

Cowboy State Lawmen: Duty and Honor

Wyoming Mountain Investigation
Wyoming Ranch Justice
Wyoming Undercover Escape
Wyoming Christmas Conspiracy
Wyoming Double Jeopardy
Corralled in Cutthroat Creek

Cowboy State Lawmen

Wyoming Winter Rescue
Wyoming Christmas Stalker
Wyoming Mountain Hostage
Wyoming Mountain Murder
Wyoming Cowboy Undercover
Wyoming Mountain Cold Case

Visit the Author Profile page at Harlequin.com.

CAST OF CHARACTERS

Nora Santana—Years ago, she escaped the clutches of a serial killer and has never fully recovered. She's desperate to put the past behind her but must confront it if she hopes to ever have a future.

Bo Lennox—A former Air Force combat engineer turned private investigator with Ironside Protection Services who must use all his skills to keep Nora safe.

Chance Reyes—He's a sharp attorney and in charge of the Ironside Protection Services office in Big Sky Country.

Logan Powell—He's a detective with the Bitterroot Falls Police Department.

Autumn Stratton—She's a criminal profiler and investigator for Ironside Protection Services.

Declan Hart—He's a special agent with DOJ Division of Criminal Justice.

Jackson Powell—He's a US marshal in Missoula.

Chapter One

Nora Santana caught sight of a red and gold envelope glittering in the snow on her doorstep.

An icy chill skittered down her spine that had nothing to do with the nip in the December evening air. She stopped on her walkway, clutching her keys tight in her gloved hand, and glanced around.

The block was quiet. All the single-family homes were spread far apart, sitting on lots that exceeded three acres. Which was what she preferred. It made it easy to see any neighbors or someone who didn't belong on her property, yet still be close enough for someone to hear her scream for help if the need ever arose.

The neighborhood was decorated for the holidays, with every house adorned in cheerful lights and festive displays. Her home, the only one at the end of the cul-de-sac near the woods, was dark and lonely. It stood out for all the wrong reasons.

She hated this time of year, ever since she was sixteen and escaped.

Survived.

Nora stared at the envelope, her pulse fluttering. The fresh snow on the walkway and stairs was pristine, devoid of any footprints, as if someone had meticulously erased them. The peculiarity struck her as odd.

Taking one last look around, she climbed the four steps of her porch and picked up the envelope and read the typed message.

To Nora
From Your Secret Santa

It was probably left by one of her neighbors, she told herself. A gift card from Mrs. Moore would be her guess. The older lady was fond of Nora. Each Christmas, the sweet woman tried to get Nora to celebrate the holiday, but always failed. In the past, her kind neighbor had dropped off peppermint fudge, gingerbread sandwich cookies and eggnog Bundt cake. Nora had brought all of the treats into the real estate company where she worked and shared them with the other agents, Amanda and Joe, since there was no one else in her life. Last week, Nora had several lengthy conversations with her neighbor about the holiday and finally mustered the courage to politely ask the older woman not to make anything else for her this year. Mrs. Moore had looked disappointed, but she had agreed.

Nora tucked the envelope in her pocket.

Although Christmas was still two weeks away, her widowed neighbor planned to spend the holiday with her son in Helena. She was going to leave in a few days to enjoy her grandkids.

Nora had started marking her time in Bitterroot Falls, Montana, with Mrs. Moore's gifts.

Four years. This was the longest she'd stayed in one place since...

She shuddered, stomach churning.

Razor-sharp images slashed through her mind—an onslaught of memories. Of stark fear. Pain. Bone-chilling screams.

The sensation of pins and needles flared in her fingers, crawling into her hands and up her arms. Her pulse spiked, heartbeat drumming in her ears. Nora squeezed her eyes shut and took deep breaths to stave off a panic attack. Inhaled, exhaled, and repeated until it passed.

Nearly a decade ago, her life had been irrevocably changed, the future she'd imagined smashed into a billion little pieces. She shoved the searing memories from her mind, back into the buried vault that she never dared touch.

Opening her eyes, she unlocked her front door and stepped inside the house. Immediately the rhythmic beeping of her alarm sounded, alerting her that she had thirty seconds to disarm it before the security company called. Kicking off her boots, she closed the door, flipped the dead bolt and slipped on the chain. She moved to the system's panel on the wall and entered the code. The alarm went silent. Then the small red light flashed, showing the system was set for the night.

Fatigue seeped through her. The day had been longer than she'd expected with multiple house showings. After Halloween, the real estate market typically slowed down to a crawl, but she had two motivated sellers. They were both eager to offload their properties before the new year. Also, a family in the process of relocating to Bitterroot had a severe case of the Goldilocks syndrome. Every house they toured was either too big or too small, too outdated or too new. The picky family only wanted something that was just right.

Her stomach growled. She trudged to the kitchen, then set down her laptop bag and purse on the countertop of the eat-in island. Her left shoulder ached terribly, even though it had been seven weeks since her injury, when she was shot. A victim in a mass shooting on Main Street.

She was still struggling to get back full range of motion.

You're better. Every day it hurts less and you can do more. Be thankful you're still breathing.

The physical therapist explained the tenderness would continue for a while but assured Nora a full recovery and return to normal would happen.

Nothing in her life had been normal in a long, long time even before the shooting. At least she was able to jog again, though running in the snow was more taxing on her body. She stretched through the discomfort.

Pain was a good reminder that she was alive. That she could endure anything.

She took the red and gold envelope from her pocket and tore it open. Maybe it was a gift card to the local café, The Beanery. Not that Mrs. Moore should've gone through the trouble after Nora had made it clear that she didn't want to celebrate the holidays. Her neighbor knew Nora spent way too much money in the café—or used to anyway. She hadn't been back to Main Street since the gunman had opened fire in broad daylight.

Nora pulled the card out of the envelope and froze.

Intricate drawings lined the border, images repeating over and over. Santa Claus, an angel and a devil. Typed across the center of the card were three lines that read:

No more running.
Hide and Seek is over.
Time for a new game.

Nora's skin crawled as her stomach tangled into sickening knots.

No, no, no.

He found me.

After years of hiding, of trying to be invisible, her worst fears were crystallizing.

The room spun. She struggled to focus. To breathe. The serial killer, who had murdered her friends ten years ago, who had almost taken her life, too, had finally found her.

Now he was going to make good on his promise.

To finish what he'd started.

The card in her hand was shaking because she was trembling. Everywhere. She dropped the note onto the counter. Clenched her hands together in a tight fist. Rubbed her knuckles with her interlocked fingers.

Breathe. Think.

Her cell phone rang, and she jumped. Snatching the phone from her coat's pocket, she glanced at the screen. A random number she didn't recognize.

Another telemarketer. She was in no mood to deal with it. "Hello," she answered, sharply, prepared to keep the conversation short.

"Sweet Nora. It's been far too long." The voice was deep. Eerie. Electronically modified.

Dread flooded her system, and her pulse ratcheted higher. It was him. He'd not only found her and had her address, but also her private cell number. She opened her mouth to speak, but her throat tightened, growing so dry as though filled with sand. No words would come out.

She sagged against the counter.

"Nor-a, Nor-a," he said in a singsongy way, the all too familiar cadence setting every nerve in her body on edge. "Let's play Santa Says."

Panic fired up inside her, burning and roiling. Rage bubbled to the surface. "Drop dead!"

Laughter, dark and devoid of humor, rolled over the

phone line. "No one dies tonight. My game. My rules. Santa says, don't call the police. Or. Else."

Hot bile spurted up the back of her throat and she swallowed it down. "Or else what?"

"Or else we'll have to play a different game. A painful game. A very bloody game."

A decade of grief knocked her sideways as the horrific screams of her friends filled her ears. This monster had tortured them before he killed them. Stabbed each of them several times before ending their misery.

Tears burned the backs of her eyes, and her stomach churned. Shaking her head, she squeezed the bridge of her nose and stared down at the note on the counter. She needed to breathe. Needed to think.

"Oh, sweet Nor-a. Don't look so sad. Playing Santa Says will be such fun."

His words echoed in her mind. *Don't look so sad.*

She snapped her head up and glanced around. The house was locked up tight, with the alarm on, yet she wondered if he was somehow watching her.

Unzipping her purse, she snatched the Beretta that was inside. Clutched the cold metal against her chest. She felt a grim reassurance mixed with the sobering realization that ultimately it wouldn't save her. The nature of his games, the structure of his rules, all designed for her to lose and for him to win.

She spun around, rushing to the kitchen sink. Easing back the curtains, she peeked outside. Darkness stretched across the lawn to the perimeter of Mrs. Moore's home. Moonlight reflected off the glistening sheet of untouched snow. Colored string lights hung from the eaves of the house. No large shrubs or trees for anyone to hide behind.

"Nor-a." The electronic modification only amplified the

creepiness of his voice. "You won't need a gun for Santa Says. Put it down on the counter."

She stilled, blood pounding in her ears. Her thoughts coalesced into the horrifying reality of her situation. He *was* watching.

Spying on her.

"Where are you?" she asked, the Beretta shaking in her hand.

"Close. Much closer than you realize. But not close enough for you to use the gun."

Terror pulsed like a feverish drumbeat in her veins. She rounded the island and hurried to the back door. It had a steel frame with two large panels made of tempered glass. She'd never put up curtains. Since the door faced the woods rather than a neighbor's house, she hadn't thought she needed them.

Frost streaked the windowpanes. Nora scanned the yard, searching for any signs of him. Nothing. Not a single footprint marred the blanket of pristine snow, though that meant little.

She watched and waited for any movement.

Still nothing.

But a sudden prickle along her arms and back made her stare even harder into the darkness. Her fingers gripped the edge of the doorframe, and her other hand tightened around the gun.

A shadow flitted in the moonlight between two evergreens at the tree line.

She held her breath, her gaze glued to the spot. *There*.

Movement again.

The shadow stepped out into view. Black clothing. A ball cap on his head. His face shrouded in darkness. He waved at her, and she shivered.

"Hello, Nora."

Her teeth chattered, but not from the cold. A rolling tremor had started in her jaw and now slithered through her body.

How long had he been watching her? Hours? Days? *Weeks?*

The entire time she'd been on display in the back part of her house. In her bedroom upstairs that also overlooked the woods. Where she got dressed and walked around with no clothes on. While he was watching her. Planning his next move—this moment.

Fear clogged her throat and paralyzed her muscles.

"Put the gun down on the counter," he said.

Playing his game, on his terms, meant that when he was done toying with her and it was over, she'd die.

There was only one option.

One choice.

Fight back with everything she had until her last breath. Nora grabbed the door handle, aching to run outside and unload every single bullet into him.

Maybe that was what he wanted. For her to turn off the alarm. To leave the safety of the house. To chase after him all the while he was taunting her.

"Santa says do it now," he said.

She backed away from the door.

"Good girl. Go to the counter and set down the gun."

Instead, she ran to the other security panel mounted on the wall.

"What are you doing?" he demanded.

Keeping the Beretta in her hand, she looked back through the glass, hoping he could see her face, and pressed the panic button on the security panel, holding it for three seconds.

The alarm activated, blaring. The police would soon be dispatched.

"I warned you!" he said, over the screeching alarm. "Now I'll make you suffer!"

She tightened her grip on the gun and stepped up to the back door.

The shadowy figure stood there, breathing heavily over the line, waiting for a response from her that she refused to give.

She was done giving him her fear and her pain and her weakness. Done playing by his rules.

No more.

"Mark my words, *Noriyah*. You'll regret this!"

She'd changed her name, her hair, stayed away from her family and friends over the years. She'd taken every precaution. All for what?

He found her anyway. Again.

The killer disconnected the call and backed away into the darkness of the woods.

No relief came to her. This wasn't over. Far from it. This was only the beginning of a new deadly nightmare.

He was going to keep coming after her until one of them was dead.

Nora swore to herself that it wasn't going to be her.

Chapter Two

"Conference room, now," his boss said, stopping in the doorway of his office.

Bo Lennox looked up from his computer screen at Chance Reyes, a growl of irritation rising in his chest. "What's up?"

Tall, tanned, and with a relaxed, posh air that made him appear far younger than he was, Chance looked like he belonged at a fancy law firm—he was an attorney after all—or hobnobbing at a country club. "We have a potential new client. I want you and Autumn to sit in on the interview," Chance said, referring to Ironside Protection Services' newest team member, a forensic psychologist and former FBI consultant turned investigator.

Dr. Autumn Stratton was sharp, had a keen way of pinpointing a perp and had proven she also had guts. Although she was still learning the ropes at IPS, she'd become an essential part of the crew.

"Just us two?" Bo asked.

Chance gave a curt nod.

Since his boss wasn't bringing the other two guys on the team—Takoda Yazzie and Eli Easton—to the meeting, Bo wondered about the nature of the case and whether Autumn's expertise was truly necessary or if this was an opportunity for her to gain more experience.

More importantly, why had he been picked?

"I just finished a case," Bo said. It had been a security nightmare. "I was only planning to be in the office for a couple of hours to close out this paperwork." He'd been hoping to take some downtime. Go skiing. Mountain climbing. Kick back with a beer in front of the fire and unwind. "Why not grab Eli or Tak?"

"Because the client asked for you."

Bo straightened. "Me?"

"Yeah," Chance said. "She requested that you sit in on the meeting."

She. "Okay."

After slipping on the sport coat that he kept in the office for meetings such as these, Bo grabbed a notepad and pen and hurried behind Chance to the conference room near the front of their office spaces. Autumn was already sitting inside speaking with Nora Santana.

Bo faltered to a stop. He remembered her. How could he not? The young woman was unforgettable.

She turned toward the door. The second her gaze lifted to lock with his, he forgot how to breathe. How to think.

Then she smiled at him, and he was certain that was what it must've felt like to be struck by lightning.

She wasn't pretty, nor was she simply beautiful. She was a knockout.

Caramel complexion. Delicate features and sensual lips. Petite, dainty frame.

A soft powder blue cashmere dress molded to her shapely body. Long dark hair hung past her shoulders in wavy curls, framing a face that was too alluring. And her eyes. Amber was too tame a color to describe her eyes. Flecked with gold in the light, they reminded him of a lion. Or perhaps it was the quiet fierceness to her.

"I believe you know Bo Lennox," Chance said, taking a seat.

She started to rise from her chair, prompting his feet to move.

He schooled his features as he approached her side of the table. "Ms. Santana." He shook her hand, surprised by her tight, firm grip.

"Please, call me Nora," she said, and he had to fight a quiver zipping down his spine because her voice was soft, yet husky, awakening every sense. She sat back down. "We should be on a first-name basis. After all, you have already seen me naked."

Lowering his gaze, Bo stepped back. "I'm sorry about that." Once again. He glanced at Chance, who had arched an eyebrow, and then at Autumn's shocked expression. "It was an accident. I interviewed her at the hospital after the mass shooting."

Seven weeks ago, a sniper had opened fire on Main Street, killing two people and wounding two others. In the incident, Nora was one of the injured, struck in the left shoulder. The shot had been clean, exiting out the other side. No serious damage had been done. No bone had been hit. She'd been lucky.

"Bo walked in while I was in the middle of changing out of my hospital gown and the timing had been perfect."

"Off," he corrected. "Bad timing."

A flush suffused her cheeks.

He lowered his head and edged toward the door.

Bo had assisted Chance and Winter Stratton—Autumn's sister that worked as an agent with the DOJ Division of Criminal Investigation—with the case, right along with the rest of the team. Bo had been the one to question Nora about the events and to see if she had any information that might help them identify the shooter.

At the emergency room, she'd been in a cubicle when he'd drawn back the curtain without thinking. He'd glimpsed flawless light brown skin, mouthwatering curves straight out of a fantasy and then a startled expression on her face before he apologized and quickly excused himself.

The only fortunate thing about his intrusion that day was that he'd stopped Nora from leaving the hospital prematurely. She'd been scared and he'd assumed it had been the shock from the shooting. After the doctors treated her and stitched up the wound, they wanted to monitor her for forty-eight hours. Bo had to persuade her to stay.

She hadn't known anything valuable about the sniper, but he'd used the circumstances to spend a little time with her, even driving her home once she was discharged.

"Nora," Chance said, "why don't you tell us what you think we can do for you?" His boss looked at Bo and gestured to a chair.

Bo shook his head. "I'm good." He leaned against the door jamb.

Nora shoved hair back behind her ear. "I'm not sure where to start."

"At the beginning is a good place," Autumn said, seated next to her.

Nora nodded. "Ten years ago, when I was sixteen, a group of us, me and three other friends, were targeted by a murderer. The press dubbed him the Yuletide Killer."

"Was he caught?" Chance asked.

"No. He murdered my three friends. I was the only one who got away." Her voice thickened with emotion. "The only one who survived."

"Take your time. There's no rush." Autumn put a hand

on her shoulder. "When you say that you got away, do you mean you were taken and escaped?"

"We were having a sleepover at Jessica's house in the basement. Her parents were out of town for a couple of nights. The killer broke in. Slaughtered Dana, Alice and Jessica. I was in the bathroom when I heard their screams. I hid in a crawl space, where Jessica stashed things that she didn't want her parents to find. I stayed down there for hours. Terrified. Not making a sound until the police found me."

As she recounted that tragic moment, tears welled in her eyes, her body trembling. The weight of her pain was etched across her face and it radiated off her. His heart ached to ease her suffering. The urge to reach out and comfort her was overwhelming, but he resisted.

"A few days later, he came back for me," she said. "He almost got me into a van while I was walking to Savvy's house."

"Savvy?" Bo asked.

"Savannah Watts. Everyone called her Savvy for short. She was my best friend. Lived around the corner. The man got a hold of me, but I managed to scream, drawing attention. Some guys were out shoveling snow from the sidewalk and ran over to help me as I fought not to be thrown into the van. I knew that if he got me inside that I was as good as dead."

"You have good instincts," Bo said. "Not letting him move you to a secondary location."

"Pa, my stepdad, always told me that. He was a cop."

"Wise advice that saved you," Chance said.

Nora grabbed the cup of coffee from the table and her hand shook as she drank a swallow. "The guilt, the shame that I had because I had lived when the others hadn't, was a lot. I went to stay with relatives in Wyoming and I finished high school there and started college. But then he found me. Tried to kill me again." She pulled down the collar of her sweater dress and moved her hair back, revealing a scar on her neck.

Everything inside Bo went cold. Rigid. The killer had gotten a rope or cord around her neck, tight enough to leave a permanent scar.

"I fought him. My roommate in the dorm, Jane, walked in," Nora said. "She came back early from a party. Screamed for help. If not for her, he would've finished me that night. But he stabbed Jane as he fled. Killed her instead. Because she had interfered with his fun. That's what he said to her as she was dying." Nora covered her neck and clutched the cup in both hands. "I was already taking self-defense classes and learning martial arts at a place called the Underground Self-Defense School. That's how I was able to fight him off at all, but I was still new to it. The woman who owned the school, Charlie, helped me change my name—from Noriyah Howard to Nora Santana—and start over."

Chance leaned forward. "Charlie Sharp, in Laramie?"

"Do you know her?" Nora asked with surprise.

Bo's boss was from Laramie, and he was the type of guy who made it his business to know everyone.

"I do," Chance said.

"I cut all contact with family after that, thinking that if I disappeared completely, he would never be able to find me. I bounced around various places, keeping up my training in self-defense and learning how to shoot. Eventually, I wanted to come back home to Montana. I have a younger half sister, Rosa, and an older stepbrother, Spencer, who I was close to. I've missed so much. When scrolling through their Facebook pages isn't enough, sometimes I drive over to Cold Harbor, where I'm from, to get a glimpse of their lives."

The small town of Cold Harbor was located in the rugged mountains, nestled deep within a remote region. It was approximately a three-hour drive away from Bitterroot Falls. Bo had passed through the mining town once or twice.

"I sit outside the church and watch them file out after service," Nora said, the loneliness in her voice gnawing at him. "Spencer and Savvy are a couple. Married for years and have a baby. Rosa got hitched, too. I've never met her husband or my niece."

"Is that how he found you?" Chance asked. "By going back home?"

"No," Bo said. "It was the shooting on Main Street. Right?"

Nora met his gaze, her eyes widening, and she nodded.

"Her face and name, right along with Ty Long's," Bo said, "the other guy who'd been shot, were all over the news." News that had received national coverage.

That day, Bo had escorted her out of the hospital to his vehicle so he could take her home. Nora had recoiled from the cameras, declining to answer any questions from the swarm of reporters that had descended on Bitterroot Falls. At the time, he'd assumed she'd been shy and simply wanted her privacy. Not that it had been an act of self-preservation.

If only he'd known the real reason for her aversion that day, he would've done a better job of protecting her.

"Things were quiet while I recovered." Nora put a hand to her shoulder and rubbed the spot of her injury like it suddenly ached. "I'd hoped he hadn't seen me on the news, but the coverage was everywhere. Almost constant for days. I guess my luck ran out because when I got home from work last night, there was a note on my front stoop," she said, bringing up pictures on her phone.

Bo walked closer to the table and peered over at the screen as she scrolled through.

A red and gold envelope. A note card. Autumn took the phone and zoomed in. Hand-drawn colorful images.

Santa was holding an open book of deeds.

An angel with a halo.

A red devil with a tail and heavy chains draped over his shoulders.

The words in the middle of the card were chilling. *No more running. Hide and Seek is over. Time for a new game.*

"After I got inside the house and opened it, I received a phone call. From him. I could tell he was watching me. I found him in the backyard, hiding in the tree line of the woods at the rear of my house." A visible shudder ran through her. "I pulled out the Beretta I carry in my purse. He wanted to play Santa Says—told me not to call the police and to put my gun down. Instead of playing his twisted game, I notified the police. That's what brought me here. The cops couldn't help me. There were no prints on the card and the man in the woods hadn't done anything illegal. No proof it was even the killer."

"Did you recognize his voice on the phone?" Bo asked.

"He used a voice modulator. The same as he's always done in the past. I've never seen his face. Not ten years ago, not that night in my dorm room and he stood too far away last night. Detective Logan Powell recommended that I hire Ironside Protection Services."

Not too long after Chance recruited Bo and the other IPS guys from a combat-ready unit at Malmstrom Air Force Base, Logan Powell and his now fiancée Summer Stratton moved to Bitterroot Falls as well. Then her sisters, Autumn and Winter—the "season sisters" as Chance called them—had followed shortly thereafter. These days they were always together, joining the IPS team for dinners, celebrations, Sunday brunches, just to have drinks and hang out. They had each other's backs through the good and bad. Cared for one another.

They'd formed a sort of family. As a foster kid, always bouncing through the system when he was younger, not having any roots or relatives, Bo relied on this newly found family more and more. Not only relied on them but appreciated them. Trusted them.

If Logan had sent Nora to IPS, then the police really couldn't do much, if anything at all, to keep her safe.

"It creeped me out to stay at my house last night now that he knows where I live. I felt..." Nora wrung her hands. "Exposed there, too vulnerable. I spent the night at the hotel in town. The Bitterroot Mountain Hotel. That was hard too because the sniper had been on the hotel rooftop the day he shot up Main Street. I hadn't been back to that part of town since it happened."

"You've been through a lot recently," Autumn said. "Traumatic experiences. I'm sorry you had to revisit that area before you were ready."

"I didn't sleep at all last night. I kept checking the locks on the hotel room. Moved the dresser to block the door. But still, I couldn't relax enough to get any rest."

Bo tore his gaze from her, wanting to comfort her in some way.

Chance clasped his hands on the table. "It was smart not to stay at your house. The hotel was safer."

"Not safe enough. I found something *inside* my car this morning. Waiting for me on the passenger's seat." She picked up her messenger bag from the floor, flipped open the front flap and took out a red and gold box with a shiny red bow on top. "Do you smell it?"

They all gathered closer to the box.

Bo inhaled deeply, bracing himself for a rancid stench. It was the opposite.

"What is that?" Autumn asked.

"Cologne," Bo said.

Nora nodded, her bottom lip trembling, and his entire focus fell to her mouth. Those full, rosy lips. He wondered what it'd be like to kiss her.

"Whenever he's gotten close to me," Nora said, "that's what he smelled like. My car reeks of the scent. Of him. I drove with the windows rolled down, but it's still in there."

"The smell is woodsy." Autumn took another whiff. "Spicy. Like fire and cloves and something else."

"There's more." Nora lifted the lid of the red and gold box, revealing the contents.

A piece of coal. Sugar plums. A gold ring with a tiny accent diamond—possibly a wedding band.

And another card with the same design around the border. The typed words read:

Your punishment for not listening.
A new game.
SHARKS and MINNOWS.

"Nobody is to touch anything," Chance said. "Not until Logan takes a look at it and checks it for prints. Nora, do you recognize the ring?"

"It looks familiar." She shrugged. "But I can't place it." Exhaling a shaky breath, she wrung her hands once more. "My first instinct was to disappear again. Change my name. Start over someplace else. But I'm tired of uprooting my life. I don't want to run anymore, always looking over my shoulder. Living in constant fear that this very thing will happen. Please, help me."

"You need protection and a safe house to stay in until we can figure out who this guy is and stop him," Chance said. He looked up at Bo. "Your place is designed for this sort of thing and you have the most experience with personal security."

Bo shook his head. "No. I can't." He backed up to the doorway as all eyes in the room focused on him. "I'm not right for this one."

They all had the necessary skills as well as safe places. In fact, Chance had the most secure property. His house was located on a ranch he had turned into a compound, with lots of guys who worked there to keep watch. Not that Chance was available to handle this one. A big case was taking him out of town later that night.

"Nonsense." Chance leaned back in his chair. "You're perfect and available to start today."

"Tak or Eli would be better suited. Don't worry, Ms. Santana," Bo said to her, not looking at her mesmerizing eyes, or her lush mouth, or her face that was too wholesome, too pretty. "You'll be in good hands with someone else at IPS."

He shuffled out of the room and stalked back to his office.

No sooner had he plopped into the chair behind his desk and released a heavy breath than Chance strode into his office and shut the door.

"I realize you just wrapped up a tough case, but that's not like you." Chance folded his arms and studied him. "What's going on? Give it to me straight."

Unfiltered blunt talk was one of the things he enjoyed about working for IPS and specifically Chance. Nonetheless, this wasn't something he wanted to discuss. "I don't want this one. Ask E or Tak. All right?"

"No, it's not all right. 'I don't want to' is not an acceptable response. I hate to pull rank here, but I will. I don't ask, I assign. The client requested you, so you're on this unless you give me a solid reason to reconsider."

Bo weighed his options but didn't see any way around telling him the truth. "I can't work on her case because I'm attracted to her. Okay?" Embarrassment burned through him at having disclosed so much.

Chance grinned. "Is that all?"

Quite a lot if you asked Bo. More than enough to recuse himself. "It'd be a distraction. This job demands we don't let our attention stray." Not even for a minute. She needed someone laser-focused on keeping her safe, not juggling conflicting agendas—protecting her and getting cozy with her.

"Can you keep it in your pants?"

Bo stiffened. "Yes." He prided himself on self-restraint, but every time he looked at Nora, he wanted to touch her. Get closer to her. Kiss her. Keeping it in his pants wasn't the problem. Being near her was. It was impossible for him to focus clearly on anything other than Nora Santana when he was in the same room as her. "But it's not worth the risk."

"Not your call to make," Chance said. "It's mine. The client requested you and I think you're the best fit. Your personal interest in her will only make you more invested in doing your job."

Bo shoved back from his desk and stood. "I disagree." She deserved someone who would be one thousand percent focused on the mission and nothing else. "Distractions cause mistakes. The wrong error could cost someone their life." He wouldn't jeopardize hers.

"This type of situation requires the client to trust the person assigned. You already have a rapport with her. One she values. That makes this case yours. Like it or not."

Eli and Tak were both engaging and friendly. Capable. Nora simply hadn't had an opportunity to get to know them. A small thing easily rectified. Either man would easily earn her trust. Do the job without endangering her.

"No," Bo said.

Straightening, Chance arched both eyebrows.

Bo never turned down any assignment. Not for any reason. He certainly didn't get into a debate with his boss unless there was an ethical basis, and Chance was more than his employer. The guy was a close friend. Family.

"You feel so strongly about this that you're prepared to quit?" Chance asked, his expression stern.

A knock on the door stopped Bo from answering.

Nora stood on the other side. She opened it and poked her head in the office. "Can I speak with Bo for a minute? Alone?"

"Certainly," Chance said and stepped outside. "I'm going to call Logan and then I'll be in the conference room." He shut the door and disappeared down the hall.

"I know you don't want to take my case." She wrapped her arms around herself. "But I'd like you to reconsider. In ten years, I haven't felt secure anywhere or at ease with anyone. After the mass shooting, you came to the hospital to question me, and you were so patient and kind. Then when you followed up to see if I'd remembered anything else and offered to take me home because I had no one else I could call, it was the first time—in a very long time—that I felt safe. Do you remember the day I left the hospital with the press swarming around the building?"

Bo nodded.

Hard to forget. Nothing as big as the mass shooting had warranted a flock of reporters from national outlets as well as news podcasters to descend on their small town of Bitterroot Falls.

In many ways, the sniper had victimized Nora twice, by shooting her and then creating such mayhem that it caused her identity and whereabouts to be exposed in the media.

"As we were leaving the hospital, walking through the parking lot, surrounded by reporters hounding me, you cut through them like a blade, got them out of my face and whisked me into the car. Even the ride home to my house was peaceful. The way you comforted me—made me feel protected, simply by being there when you didn't have to—meant a lot to me."

Bo stood behind his desk, stunned and silent. He'd only been doing his job, careful not to cross any lines after the emergency room incident. Making an impression hadn't been his intent, but he was glad he'd made a difficult time a little easier for her.

"The Yuletide Killer told me over the phone the police wouldn't be able to keep me safe. He was right. After Logan Powell referred me to Ironside Protection Services, I almost threw the card in the trash and hightailed it out of town." Emotion thickened her voice. "Please, help me." She stilled, as though doing her best not to shatter into pieces. Tears clung to the corners of her eyes, but they didn't fall as if she were holding them back with an act of sheer will. "Please."

He couldn't ignore the beaten, weary look to her—fragile instead of fierce. Bo didn't like that. She had been through hell and he wondered how much more she could handle. He found himself needing to soothe her.

This was the perfect case for IPS. Just not for him. "We will help you," he said, the words slipping from his mouth before he'd considered the repercussions. "They will. One of the others."

"The reason I didn't throw the card away was because I remembered you worked here. I don't know if IPS can do anything for me, if anyone can, but I'm willing to take a chance on you, Bo. Either you handle my case personally," she said, holding his gaze hostage, "or I'll be forced to run again. Eventually face the man who's been terrorizing me for a decade, dead set on killing me, all by myself. I have a bag packed in my trunk, a full tank of gas, a loaded Beretta and two thousand dollars in cash to avoid leaving a trail if you turn me down and I need to run. So, what's it going to be?" Hiking her chin up, she stood a bit taller, stiffening as if she was bracing for bad news. "Are you going to take my case? Or am I on my own again?"

Something inside his chest cracked open, and every drop of sound reasoning spilled away from him.

Chapter Three

Any expectations Nora might've entertained had been cast aside in favor of hope. A small seed of hope, grown out of desperation.

Sitting in the passenger's seat of Bo's full-size pickup, she glanced over at him while he drove to his place, studying the side of his face that wasn't obscured by his tan cowboy hat. Smooth mahogany skin. Ruggedly handsome with a strong jaw. Clean shaven. Ridiculously muscled body that was apparent even with the layer of a winter coat.

His expression was unreadable, his posture rigid and his demeanor bordering on aloof. It was making her reevaluate her previous impression of him at the hospital when he interviewed her. Then he'd been professional, pleasant and not much of a talker other than asking questions—reserved yet not reluctant to be in her presence.

Why had she blabbered in his office, saying all that stuff about feeling safe and at ease with him?

Well, because it had been true. Still, replaying it in her head with the silence between them thickening and expanding, it had been a misstep on her part.

Running was easy. Fighting was intuitive, and she'd trained hard in self-defense to sharpen her skills after being attacked in the dorm. But stopping the killer who was hunting her—winning—that was hard.

She'd done this on her own for so long. She was tired and unsure if she could go up against that monster again by herself and prevail. A wave of hopelessness mixed with helplessness washed over, threatening to pull her under. She had to fight the urge to burst into tears. Continuing to do this alone meant running forever. Or dying. Neither choice was acceptable, but she didn't want to drag an unwilling soul into this nightmare.

Mirrored shades hid his eyes. Nonetheless, she could tell he still didn't want to work with her. Yet, for some reason, he had relented.

"Maybe this was a mistake," she said, reconsidering. "Getting you to take this assignment." More like pressuring him into it.

His jaw worked up and down like he was chewing the tension between them.

"You don't have to do this. Really. Starting over somewhere else, with a new name, would probably work." It had been working quite effectively until the mass shooting had caused her face and name to be blasted all over the news.

"No." The single word came out as a grunt.

He didn't say anything else to assuage her guilt. Nothing to quash her doubts.

"Are you sure?" she asked, giving him another out. Running and hiding, barely living, wasn't what she wanted. But she would do whatever was necessary. She was a survivor.

He gave a firm nod. "A done deal."

Whatever the cause for him to agree and take her case, she was grateful. "How is this protection thing supposed to work? I can't be trapped in a safe house. I have a job and commitments. I promised to do the food pantry and soup kitchen tomorrow." She must've sounded high maintenance and demanding. Not the impression she wanted to give him. "I don't want that sick murderer to steal what little life I've made for myself, Bo. I've done nothing wrong and don't want to be the one locked up in a prison."

His smile was so kind that it stole her next breath. "I respect that. I've seen you around town volunteering for all sorts of things. I know it's important to you."

"You've seen me around?" *Noticed me?* "Before the shooting?"

"Yeah."

"Why haven't you ever talked to me?" Not really a fair question. She'd seen him around plenty of times and had never once bothered to introduce herself, much less have a real conversation.

Bo shrugged. "I see a lot of people around. Can't talk to everyone." He cleared his throat. "Anyway, we'll review your schedule, and you'll go about your day-to-day activities as if it's business as usual. I'll follow you. Discreetly."

It occurred to her that the way he gave in was too easy. She lifted a brow. The risks to this approach were all too apparent. "If I don't stay in the safe house and go about my life, then it's more likely he'll come for me again."

"That particular downside is true. Easier to lure him out if you're in front of him, easy to see, rather than holed up at my place."

"I guess so. It's not like I'll be unprotected. Anything to catch him."

"You're very brave."

She didn't feel brave. More like terrified.

Bo turned down a long road bracketed by woods and a house appeared in the distance. A cabin on a large piece of land.

"I thought it was better to be in a highly populated area for security reasons," she said.

"In general, it is. But I like my privacy." Bo pulled up in front of the house that sat at the end of the long road on the outskirts of town and threw the gear of the Tacoma in Park.

"Trading privacy for security isn't a luxury I've had." Striking the right balance had been the key.

She looked around at the dense woods surrounding his cabin.

Ironside Protection Services had an excellent reputation that had only grown since she'd been in Bitterroot Falls, but staying in the middle of nowhere—a remote, isolated location—defied everything she had learned over the years that had helped her stay safe.

She'd insisted on Bo protecting her based on their limited interaction—which had previously been positive, almost warm—and her instinct. That preternatural ability to know the best way to keep breathing that came to her as a little voice inside. It had never led her astray. But maybe she had confused that sixth sense with something else.

Awareness.

Attraction.

Nora didn't want to go there. Entertaining such thoughts was a different kind of torture. She led a minimalist life. She kept only the bare essentials that she could leave behind at a moment's notice if she had to. A boyfriend, having anyone she cared about deeply, would've been a sticky thread tying her to a place. The ties that bind would tempt her to stay and only get her killed.

It was instinct. That's what made me choose Bo. Nothing more.

The little voice inside snickered and whispered, *Keep lying to yourself if it makes you feel better.*

Wringing her hands, she made the voice quiet down.

"There are other considerations," he said, as if picking up on her concerns. "With lots of neighbors, it's easier for someone to get close to your house and blend in. Come up with a plausible excuse to be in the vicinity. Out here, there's no hiding. No excuses. Either you're here because I expected you or you're a threat."

That was the most he'd spoken on the entire drive.

She glanced around at the snow-covered trees and icicles that hung from branches, glistening in the sunlight. "Isn't it easy for someone to hide in the woods at night and keep watch, the way he did at my place?"

"I have motion-activated sensors and cameras in the trees in case anyone approaches from the woods instead of the road."

"Never thought of that." His level of preparation and vigilance eased her qualms. "It's smart."

"It's my job."

I have a bodyguard. Real protection for once.

Bo grabbed her bag from the backseat and hopped out of the truck. She slid down from the pickup.

Puffy white clouds rolled across the azure sky against the backdrop of the snowcapped mountains. The location, nestled in the countryside, boasted an idyllic charm that was both captivating and peaceful. Serene. But amidst the breathtaking beauty, there was an undeniable foreboding in the air.

Nora turned to the house. Even though he was out in the middle of the woods, with no neighbors around, he'd put up colored string lights around the eaves as well as two evergreens flanking the house. He was a Christmas guy.

Along the roof, she noticed a railing. "Do you have a deck up there?"

"Yeah, it's great to hang out up there in the summer. Kick back with a glass of lemonade and take in the views."

"Sounds nice."

At the door, he turned to her. "Come here. I want you to pick a six-digit code that you'll remember. Think of it as your key to get into the house. Don't choose anything personal to you like a birth date. When you see a green light flash, put it in. Ready?"

She thought about it for a minute. For her to remember it, the number had to be based on something personal, yet unobtainable through public searches. She settled on the date she became Nora Santana. The only other person who'd know it was Charlie Sharp. "I'm ready."

He hit a couple of buttons and then held one down until she saw the little green light. "Go ahead."

She entered the six-digit date on the sleek, black keypad but backward. The smart lock beeped.

"One more thing." He took out his phone, brought up an app and typed something in. The entire keypad glowed white. "Press your thumb there and hold for three seconds."

Nora did so where he indicated. Another beep followed.

"Now you have multiple ways to get into the house. You can use the code or your thumbprint." He twisted the knob, went inside and held the door open for her.

Bracing herself for more holiday decorations, she followed him into the house.

The cabin was small but cozy with an open floor plan and modern furnishings. Simple, yet sophisticated, the rustic, chic abode was a warm and welcoming retreat.

Thankfully he hadn't gone bananas with the decorations, from what she could see. Aside from a massive Christmas tree—tall enough to reach the ten-foot-high ceiling in the corner—covered in white string lights and ornaments, complete with a star and fluffy skirt, there was only a garland hanging across the fireplace mantel.

She took off her down parka, and when he did the same, she noticed the gun holstered on his hip that hadn't been there during the meeting. He took their coats and hung them on the hook near the door, along with his blazer, cowboy hat and sunglasses. Next, his shoes came off.

Not a fan of tracking dirt or snow inside a house either, she pulled hers off as well. She kept her purse tucked against her waist, clutching the shoulder strap. An old habit of having her phone and gun close at hand, especially in an unfamiliar place.

He looked at her like he was gauging her reaction to his home.

To her new safe house.

Her heartbeat ratcheted up at having his full attention, which was more than a little overwhelming.

Forcing herself to relax, she stared back into his eyes. Deep brown and fathomless. His expression was still inscrutable, making her grit her teeth.

The perfectly straight edges of his low buzz cut, his perfectly pressed white shirt and his perfectly symmetrical face with high cheekbones and sharp angles made him a striking figure that drew admiring glances wherever he went. On numerous occasions, she'd seen him strutting around town and was guilty of being an awestruck gawker, too.

A rush of heat bloomed in her cheeks, flared in her neck and slid down her spine like liquid honey. She bit her bottom lip.

"Not much to see," he said, gesturing to the house. "Feel free to look around." His voice was soft and comforting, his demeanor now one of grim acceptance.

Then he added an encouraging nod that left her feeling

closer to settled. It shouldn't have been a thing of any significance. But it was.

She strode around and he trailed behind her closely. Each space was well-defined. An area rug in the living room and dining room solidified the appearance of faux separation. There was a four-person leather sofa, a coffee table and a large TV mounted on the wall next to the wood fireplace.

In the kitchen sat a square table with chairs rather than an island, and she imagined him eating most of his meals there. The countertops were a simple quartz. All the walls were painted a neutral color.

To her surprise, the place was spotless. Nothing out of place. No dust. Not even a dish in the sink. She prided herself on being tidy, but this was next level.

Turning to the floor to ceiling windows along the wall of the living room, she took in the view of the woods and mountains. Stunning.

"I guess with no neighbors, you don't have to worry about anyone peering in. Is that why you don't have any curtains?" Window coverings seemed a necessity for her situation even if he had motion activated cameras hidden in the trees.

"I designed and oversaw the build of the cabin. I installed bullet-resistant glass with a privacy film. During the day, we can see out, but no one can see in. I didn't want anything to obstruct that view."

The view was priceless and she could see why he'd chosen this plot of land. "What about at night?"

"When the light inside the house exceeds the light outside, the privacy film is nullified, and a potential onlooker would be able to see in. Especially at night. To fix that problem, I had boxes hidden in the ceiling of the perimeter of the house with blinds in them. I prefer the look with them concealed." He pointed to the thin outline of them in the ceiling. "When the balance of light between indoors and outdoors shifts, I have them automated to roll down, but they can also be activated manually," he said, gesturing to a panel mounted on the wall.

"How did you think to do all of that?"

"I was a combat engineer. So were Tak and Eli, the other guys at IPS. Chance recruited us from our last duty station, the 819th RED HORSE Squadron out at Malmstrom Air Force Base."

The Air Force. That made sense. Explained his military bearing, the straight posture and his neatness. "RED HORSE?"

"Sorry. Rapid Engineer Deployable, Heavy Operational Repair Squadron, Engineer. Somewhat redundant I know. The unit is always wartime ready. They rapidly mobilized people, equipment, and provided heavy repair capability, construction support and combat engineering anywhere in the world. Bottom line, we facilitated the mobility of friendly forces while impeding that of the enemy."

"That's impressive. Did you see a lot of combat?"

"More than I wanted. My last two deployments were with Special Forces. Those were rough."

"How long were you in?"

"Fifteen years. I joined straight out of high school."

He appeared far younger than he really was. She guessed thirty-three. Maybe thirty-two.

"Isn't it twenty years to retirement?" she asked, wondering why he would leave early.

"Yeah. I thought I'd be a lifer, but then I met Chance Reyes and he changed my mind. The clever guy knew exactly what he was doing. Very persuasive. He'd just opened the IPS office. The owner, Rip Lockwood, another guy from Laramie actually—"

"*The* Rip Lockwood. Infamous president of the outlaw motorcycle gang The Iron Warriors?"

"I don't know about infamous or outlaw, but yes. He started his company by gainfully employing the men in his motorcycle club and branched out from there."

Iron Warriors.

Ironside Protection.

The connection was obvious in hindsight.

"I met him once," Bo said. "He was a marine. Special Forces. Sharp. No-nonsense. I liked him. Rip had offered Chance a sweet bonus for recruitment with double the money if he got vets to join since Lockwood is a veteran himself. Chance scooped us out somehow, specifically eyeing people from RED HORSE. He was upfront and told us that he'd cut us in on a generous percentage of his bonus as a new hire incentive. Chance got the three us in one fell swoop, making IPS history to be the fastest to fully staff an office with all vets."

From her brief interaction with Chance Reyes, she'd gotten the impression he was a slick, smooth talker. Then she'd learned he was also a lawyer and it all made sense, but he struck her as a good guy. "Any regrets?"

"Nope. Not a single one. I didn't want to PCS and leave Montana for another duty station. Deploying all the time was hard. Tiring. IPS is more than a job. It's a career I'm passionate about, good at and it's given me a family that I wouldn't have otherwise." He lowered his gaze like he wished he hadn't told her so much.

She should've backed off, left it alone, but she moved closer to him. "Why not? Why don't you have any other family?"

"I grew up in foster care."

Questions raced through her mind. He'd already opened

up more than he appeared comfortable with. She didn't want to push him.

Nora put her hand on his arm. Rock-hard muscle flexed along her palm beneath his shirt, and she couldn't help but curl her fingers around his sculpted bicep. "I'm sorry. I can't imagine growing up without any roots, but I do understand what it's like to go through life alone with no one to rely on, to support you, to share things with. Good or bad." A familiar ache pulsed in time with her heartbeat.

He glanced down at her hand and his expression hardened.

She lowered her palm as he moved away from her.

"You should see the rest of the house." He strode through the living room to an open door.

She peeked inside. It was a bathroom. "Only the one?"

He nodded.

"At least it's large," she said with a smile. It was huge. Two sinks with plenty of counter space. Soaking tub. Toilet tucked away in a water closet. A shower large enough to fit four people with dual rain heads, handheld wands, body jets and a built-in bench. She glanced up at the ceiling. "Are those built in speakers?"

"Yes. I'm more of a shower person."

"You like to relax in there, not just get clean?"

An uneasy nod, like she'd peeled back yet another layer he didn't want exposed. "The shower also doubles as a steam room."

"Wow," she said. "You really put a lot of thought into every detail." The house had been carefully crafted to fit his lifestyle.

He steered her to the room on the left. "This was the guest room."

Which he had turned into an office. Or rather a command

center. There were three large screens on the long desk, in addition to a computer and lots of gadgets.

It shouldn't have been surprising since providing protection services was what he did for a living, but it was.

He sat behind the desk and typed on the keyboard, waking the monitors. "I don't keep the system activated unless I have a reason." A series of codes flew across the screen in time with the clacking of his typing. Tiny screens popped up on the three large monitors. Each showed a different part of the property. Front of the house. Left and right sides. Rear. The road leading up to the house. Various shots of the empty woods, where he had cameras mounted. Thorough coverage of the place. Bo handed her a tablet. "With that, you can see everything I can see from in here. Just power it on. You'll see a green button to 'monitor system' and tap it. That simple."

"Thanks."

She tucked the tablet under her arm as he spun out of the chair. Bo was back in the hallway beside her.

Moving to the room on the right, he shoved the door open wider. "This is the primary."

Her gaze fell to the king-size bed and dark walnut furniture that matched the hardwood floors.

It was also the only other room.

"Where am I supposed to sleep?" she asked.

"In here." He gestured to the bed.

Her lips parted on a sigh and she stared up at him wide-eyed.

"I'm going to put on fresh sheets," he said quickly. "I promise it'll be comfy."

Fresh sheets? She wasn't concerned about the bedding. "I'm supposed to sleep in here…with you?"

Shaking his head, he averted his gaze. "Oh, no, no. Of course not. I'll be out on the sofa."

"Is it a pullout?" Didn't look like one to her, but they were making them sleek these days.

"No, but it's long enough to fit me. Comfortable. Eli slept on it a few times after having too many beers when we've watched a game."

"I can't impose and have you sleeping on the sofa. I didn't realize—"

"Nora, stop," Bo cut her off, meeting her gaze, his voice deep and commanding.

The authority ringing in his tone shouldn't have been so appealing since she hated others having any power over her. Really, she did. But she couldn't ignore the tingles that danced over her skin at the way he'd spoken her name.

She raised her chin, looking back at him. "Okay. I just didn't want to put you out."

He watched her warily. "You're the client. It's not an imposition. This is my job."

So he kept reminding her.

A soft beeping sounded throughout the house, almost like a chime, repeating over and over.

"What is that?" she asked. "The alarm?"

"That sound means someone is coming down the road," he said, ducking back into the office. "It'll beep for ten seconds." Almost on cue the noise stopped. "If someone was getting close to the house by approaching from the woods, then the alarm would go off. It's a different sound. Much louder." He scanned the monitors, and she looked alongside him. A pickup truck was headed down the driveway. A silver Dodge Ram. "It's okay. A friend."

She followed him through the house. By the time they reached the living room, she heard the vehicle pulling up to the house. A car door slammed, heavy footfalls resounded up the stairs and then a hard pounding on the door made her flinch.

Bo was already at the front of the house. He glanced through the peephole—she supposed out of habit—and opened the door. Logan Powell stood on the other side.

"Come on in," Bo said.

Why was the detective here?

Logan stepped inside, but stayed on the wide doormat, apparently familiar with Bo's unspoken no shoes policy. "Hey. Chance asked me to get the police file on the Yuletide Killer from the Cold Harbor PD. They were quick to respond. I sent it to him along with the hotel security footage of the perp breaking into Nora's car. Unfortunately, we couldn't make a positive ID. I believe Chance is forwarding everything to the entire team."

"You didn't come all the way out here to tell us that," Bo said. A statement, not a question.

"No, I didn't." The detective removed his Stetson and raked a hand through his blond hair, his expression turning grim. "The ring that was in the box left for you... We believe we know who it belonged to. This morning, your neighbor, Mrs. Denise Moore, was found dead."

Nora rocked back on her heels, the words hitting her like a physical blow. "Murdered?"

"I'm afraid so."

"She was..." Her voice failed her a moment. "She was my friend." Mrs. Moore and her coworkers were the closest she had to friends. They cared about her and she cared about them.

Bo's eyes had gone steely hard. A muscle ticked in his cheek. "How was she killed?"

"I've never seen so much blood at a crime scene before,"

Logan said. His jaw clenched. He looked down at the hat in his hands. "He did unspeakable things to her. Killed her slowly. A neighbor reported blood in her driveway and that she didn't answer her door after he and his wife knocked loudly. The guy went around to the side of the house and peeked through a window. Saw the scene. Retched in the yard. Called 911."

Her chest tightened. She could barely breathe.

"Poor Mrs. Moore. She was so sweet and warm. Her son and grandkids are expecting her. She was supposed to leave to visit them tomorrow." A sob lodged in her throat, choking her. "He warned me. That monster told me that if I didn't play Santa Says, that there would be a new game." Sharks and Minnows. "A painful one. A game that will get very, very bloody."

Reality barreled through her hopeful facade, smashing it into bits. Terror and grief filled her heart. She was trapped in a horror movie. The killer would never stop. Not until she was dead. Tears filled her eyes, blurring her vision

Bo wrapped his arms around her, pulling her into a tight hug against his solid frame, and Nora realized she was shaking.

Resting her head on his chest, she breathed in through her nose and out through her mouth to loosen the knot in her throat and quell the rising tide of nausea that was swelling into a tsunami. "He told me I'd regret not playing his game." *He was right.* "And now she's dead." A sob slipped from her lips. "Mrs. Moore is dead because of me."

Chapter Four

Bo toggled from the cold case report back to the hotel security footage on his laptop and hit Play for the tenth time. A hood covered the back of the perp's head. The guy was around six feet tall with boots on—average build—and he kept his face turned away from the security cameras. He was in and out of Nora's car in less than sixty seconds.

A noise snagged Bo's attention. It came from inside the house. He pulled out the one earbud he'd been using to listen to jazz while he worked—the music helped him focus. He got up from his chair at the kitchen table and stepped into the hallway. The door to the primary bedroom was closed. He listened and heard nothing.

He would've sworn Nora was moving around, but no sound came from the bedroom. She was still resting.

Exhaling with relief, he sat back down at the handmade oak table in the kitchen.

For most of the day, she had been inconsolable, believing she was responsible for her neighbor's murder. The shock and guilt consumed Nora, and she seemed convinced she could have somehow prevented the tragedy. Bo had been at a loss about how to ease her conscience and make her feel any better. Hugging her tightly, holding her hand, offering words of reassurance—none of it did any good. Despite his best efforts, her tears kept flowing, along with her self-recrimination. Exhausted, she had showered and retreated to the bedroom to lie down.

Picking up his cell phone, he checked the state-of-the-art security app that he had downloaded. Prior to having Nora stay with him, he'd never had a need to have it on his phone. As he swiped through the interface, he noticed that all the lights on the app glowed a reassuring shade of green. The security system was functioning flawlessly and there were no signs of any movement near the house, giving him peace of mind.

However, he wasn't at ease for long. With a deep breath, he turned back to the cold case that had plagued his thoughts since he opened the e-mail from Chance. Carefully, he read through the police report once again, determined to uncover any missed clues that could bring closure to Nora's decade-long nightmare.

He stared at a picture of the note card that had been left at the crime scene. It was similar to the one sent to Nora, with the same hand-drawn images lining the border—except there was blood splattered on it and a single word typed in the center in all caps.

NAUGHTY.

The report detailed the exhaustive investigation carried out by the detectives. They had questioned every person connected to the case. Family members, friends, high school staff and even neighbors of Nora's and the three murdered teenage girls had been subjected to intense scrutiny.

No stone had been left unturned, or so it seemed. The detectives interrogated anyone who might have had a connection to the victims. Despite their tireless efforts, however, the investigation had yielded no concrete leads, no suspects, no motives beyond the sick thrill of a killer.

The murderer had gotten away scot-free with a heinous crime. Why take the risk of stalking Nora? Was he obsessed with her? Or was it because she was the only one who got away, and he refused to let her go? Or was there some other reason?

Bo scrolled through the file and found the numbers to two detectives that had been assigned to the case. One, Stacey Gagliardi, had more thorough reports and had questioned Nora's stepfather, Frank Howard, on her own several times.

On a hunch, he dialed the number for Detective Gagliardi, hoping it was still good.

It rang and rang and rang. Sighing, he prepared to leave a message that would probably never be returned.

"Hello," a woman finally answered when he thought it would go to voice mail.

"Is this Detective Gagliardi?"

"It is. Who's asking?"

"My name is Bo Lennox. I'm a private investigator with Ironside Protection Services in Bitterroot Falls. We've been hired to protect Noriyah Howard. We have reason to believe that the Yuletide Killer has found her and is stalking her again, with the intent of finishing what he started years ago."

The detective swore. "I saw her on the news a couple of months back. She was a victim of a mass shooting. Goes by the name Nora Santana now, right?"

"Yes, ma'am. That's correct."

"I wondered if he would come for her. Or if it was finally over. It had been so long, I had hoped that she would be okay, but then I heard the Bitterroot Falls PD had requested a copy of the file. I've been reexamining the case in my head all day. What can I do for you?"

"Detective Logan Powell made the request and shared the file with IPS. I've been reviewing it and had a few questions."

"I'm not sure how much help I can be after all this time," she said, sounding weary, "but go ahead, fire away."

Bo looked down at the notes he had made and started in no particular order. "You interviewed everyone close to the girls who were murdered as well as Nora, except for her biological father. Why is that?"

"The father, Jamal Banks, was living in Canada at the time—had been for several years prior—and he had no active relationship with Noriyah or her mother. I knew him. He used to be a corrections officer at the state prison. He's a Mountie now, like Dudley Do-Right. We had no reason to look into him."

"Nora mentioned having a best friend around that time. Savannah Watts. Do you know why the Watts girl wasn't at the slumber party the night of the murder?"

"If memory serves correctly, she wasn't invited. I believe the girl who was having the party, Jessica Graham, didn't get along with Savannah. But even if Savannah had been invited, she wouldn't have gone because she had the flu. The only reason Noriyah ended up going was because her bestie was sick. We spoke to Savannah the day after the murders, and I remember she didn't look good. The father took Savannah's temperature while we were there. I noticed it. Discreetly, of course. She was running a 101 fever. The illness was legitimate."

"Even though she wasn't invited to the party, did you look into Savannah's parents?"

"Sure did. The mother had been a nurse, a real pillar of the community until she got pancreatic cancer. She died before the murders. The father, Terry, used to be a cop. An accident ended his career, left him disabled. He needs a cane to walk now. Terry was home taking care of Savannah that night and her older brother Dylan was out at a party."

Bo referred back to his list of questions on the screen. "Jessica's parents were out of town that night. Any reason to suspect them? Did they make a habit out of leaving her alone?" The murders had taken place in the Graham house, yet there wasn't much in the case file on the parents.

"They left to attend a wedding. Spent two nights in Missoula. There was one thing that wasn't in my report. The father had a life insurance policy on his wife and Jessica."

"For how much?"

"A hundred thousand each."

Not enough to get rich but plenty to raise eyebrows. "Why did you leave it out of your report?"

"At the time, Jessica's father, Keith Graham, was mayor. My captain deemed the wedding a tight alibi and didn't want the existence of the insurance policy to unduly taint the case. When the perp went after Noriyah and tried to abduct her, my boss considered it proof that the mayor was not behind it. I disagreed but was ordered to drop Graham as a suspect."

Bo made several notes on the document he had opened on his laptop. The life insurance policy could be seen as questionable or practical depending on perspective. What troubled him more was the captain's insistence to eliminate Keith Graham prematurely as a potential suspect.

"It looks like you questioned Nora's stepfather several times," Bo said. "More than anyone else." The detective had put him under the microscope of suspicion for months. "Why is that?"

"For one, Frank's a former cop. He had retired a couple of years before the murders. You know who makes the best criminal? A cop. Hate to say it, but it's true. We know what our own are going to look for, how to cover our tracks, make evidence disappear. Second, I didn't trust his alibi that night of the triple homicide, when only his stepdaughter survived, that he was with his other children."

Bo glanced at the report. Son, Spencer, and daughter, Rosalinda, ages twenty-one and eleven at the time. They'd be thirty-one and twenty-one respectively today.

"Rosa said she was asleep. The son claimed to be in his room watching movies and had seen his dad in the house periodically. The thing is—Spencer and Dylan were close friends, even though the Watts boy was a little older. Thick as thieves. The same as Savannah and Noriyah. So why wasn't Spencer at the party with Dylan? When I asked him, Spencer lied. Right to my face."

Why lie? What was he hiding? "What about Nora's mom?"

"The mother, Luisa, was deceased by then. Killed in a car accident. Shortly after Spencer gave us an alibi for his father, Frank greased the wheels to get the kid hired as a cop. Fast-tracked ahead of a long waiting list of more qualified individuals, and off Spencer went to the police academy. Almost like Frank didn't want us asking him any more questions."

"Spencer's a cop, too? Seems like half the town is."

"In Cold Harbor, you're a cop, corrections officer at the state prison, coal miner or work in the service industry. The first three pay better than the last. I'm not saying that Frank helped Spencer in exchange for covering for him. But the timing was suspicious. You know what I mean? Not only that but Frank was hiding something during that investigation. So was Spencer. I'm one hundred percent positive about that. What it was that either was hiding, I may never know."

"What did your partner think?"

Gagliardi sighed. "Karl thought the only thing Frank was guilty of was being an alcoholic."

That might have been true, but cops also had a tendency to defend other cops, especially in small towns like Cold Harbor or Bitterroot Falls.

"After his wife, Luisa, died," Gagliardi continued, "Frank started hitting the bottle hard. He'd show up blitzed, reeking of booze. He hung on to his badge for two more years and then he was given a choice. Retire or be fired."

"What were the circumstances surrounding the car accident that killed Luisa?" Bo asked.

"Fourteen years ago, the Howards and Watts were together at dinner. Couples' night out. The two families were close. They'd all been drinking. Luisa was behind the wheel because she'd only had a glass of wine. Crashed the car. She was killed on impact. That was also the accident that ended Terry's career when he severely injured his leg."

"Do you know if Frank is still drinking or if he ever got help?"

"Looks like he's cleaned up his act. Heard he's been sober for a while now. Ever since Spencer got married and had a baby. I guess becoming a grandparent changed him for the better."

Bo glanced at his notes. "Did you ever have any theories about the killer's motive?"

"No. We never found any other than that creepy note with one word on it, *naughty*. Parents were afraid to leave their teens home alone after that. My partner, Karl, floated the idea that it was a nut job on a killing spree. The captain went with it. Once Noriyah moved to Wyoming and we had no other leads, we closed the case. In the end, we lacked the evidence to identify a prime suspect and to make an arrest." She huffed. "I really don't know what more I can tell you."

"Thank you for your time, Detective. I appreciate it."

"If you need anything else, don't hesitate to reach out."

"Will do. Happy holidays." Bo hung up and absorbed the details of the case and the information Detective Gagliardi shared with him.

Compiling his notes into a report for the team would help him process everything. For now, he couldn't help but feel a mix of frustration and determination. The absence of any solid leads only fueled his resolve to solve the perplexing case. Unearthing the truth behind the night that a monster claimed the lives of three teenage girls might be the only way to get justice.

Closing the report, he leaned back against his chair, the wood groaning beneath him. His mind buzzed with a sense of purpose. He knew that the answers he sought were hidden somewhere within the depths of the cold case, and he was determined to uncover them.

The bedroom door creaked open. Nora padded barefoot into the kitchen. She straightened the sweats and oversize T-shirt she'd put on. With her curly hair tousled and wild, she looked groggy. Sexy.

Yawning, she stretched as she came into the kitchen and he could tell she wasn't wearing a bra beneath the shirt. Watching her, he got the impression of a feline. Sinuous and elegant. There was nothing blatant or deliberate about her movement. Yet, she had a sensual allure he found captivating.

"You slept," he said, giving her a tentative smile. "I hope I didn't wake you. I tried to be quiet."

"I didn't hear a peep." She smiled back and set her cell phone on the table. "Thank you. For taking my case. I was able to sleep a little because I knew you were out here protecting me."

Warmth tickled his chest. "Are you hungry?"

"Did you just hear my stomach growl?"

"No, but you didn't eat anything all day. How does pizza sound to you?"

"Great."

"I always order from Giorgio's." He picked up his phone and hit the number to call them.

"You must eat a lot of pizza if you have them on speed dial."

He stiffened at how she had picked up on that small detail. There wouldn't be much he'd be able to get past her. That thought made him squirm just a bit.

"Giorgio's, how can I help you?" the hostess asked.

"What do you want?" he whispered to Nora.

"Anything is fine with me," she said, and he frowned, not believing her. "Really. I'll eat anything."

"Order for delivery." He gave the hostess his phone number, and they verified his address.

"What can I get for you?" the woman on the other end asked.

"One large mushroom and spinach with two side salads."

"Okay. That'll be one hour."

"Let the driver know there's a ten-dollar tip for him if he can deliver it in less than thirty minutes."

"I will."

He hung up.

"Big spender," Nora said.

"The delivery driver is always the same guy. Jeremy. He's a college kid who really relies on tips. I like to do what I can to help him."

"It's nice of you to do that. Little things can make a big difference."

She reached over and covered his hand with both of hers.

Her palms were warm, her hands small, but also so capable. This woman had faced danger and death multiple times and still chose to fight. Even when she ran, she made sure she protected herself, taking self-defense classes, changing her name, pulling away from those she loved most. A huge sacrifice. That took strength and courage.

So did walking into his office, looking him straight in the eye, and pushing him to personally handle her case.

They didn't say anything for a long moment as the heat from her skin seeped into him. It felt good. Nice. Bo couldn't remember the last time he'd been touched like this. Her affection, no, her kindness singed him with heat.

He wanted to take the warmth and tenderness she offered.

But he kept crossing the line with her and needed to get it together. Tearing his gaze from hers, he pulled his hands into his lap.

"At the IPS office, no one explained how this is supposed to work with the expenses, like the pizza," she said. "We didn't discuss fees. I didn't even sign a contract."

"Don't worry about anything. I'll keep track of all expenses and IPS will reimburse me. As for you, you won't owe us a dime. Chance decided this will be pro bono."

A look of perplexed surprise crossed her face. "I don't understand. Why?"

"Chance works very hard to bring in wealthy clients, so that when we have a special situation, such as yours, we can afford to do it pro bono."

"I can afford to pay. Maybe not your standard fee, not that I'm entirely sure what it is, but I don't need charity. Someone else with more limited resources than I have might need your services. Surely you can't take on every deserving case free of charge."

She was a good person with a big heart.

He'd already suspected as much about her. "Each situation is unique. Chance makes the call on how we handle it, or if we do at all. But not every case is as dire as yours."

"You mean most of your clientele don't have a serial killer stalking them?" Her tone was light, but her eyes were somber.

"Honestly, you're the first. I can't imagine anyone more deserving of our services free of charge than you."

She pursed her lips. "Can I ask you something?"

"Of course."

A curious glint flickered in her eyes, making him think of a lioness prowling the grasslands.

"If what you told me is true," she said, her voice soft, her gaze piercing, "that you can't imagine anyone being more deserving of IPS services, then why didn't you want to help me? I practically had to twist your arm into it."

A taut silence fell between them.

For several strained beats of his heart, he sat there, staring at her, with no clue how to answer. He decided to tell her the truth.

Chapter Five

Bracing herself for his answer, Nora stared at Bo.

"I didn't think I'd be the best fit for your situation," he said.

The response told her nothing, and she suspected that it had been his plan. "Why not?" she asked, digging deeper.

His lips twitched and he clenched his jaw. "It's nothing bad about you. I, um, I'd prefer not to say. A personal reason. Is that okay?"

She nodded slowly. "It is. Living the way that I have, hiding, not getting close to people, has made me very good with boundaries," she said, dropping it. He looked relieved. "I just hope this assignment won't get you into trouble with your girlfriend." She cringed inside that she had been too obvious with her question. Was he single? Or did he keep putting up a wall between them because he was involved with someone?

Normally, she was the one to shy away from questions and lingering glances and any touch that made her feel, but whenever she was near him, there was a magnetic pull tugging her toward him. The idea of getting close to anyone frightened her, but the thrill of being in his proximity was stronger.

"No trouble to worry about," he said. "I had a girlfriend

back when I was still in the Air Force, but after I got out, she left because of her change of duty station, and I didn't want a long-distance relationship. It came to a natural end."

"No one in your life since?" she asked, trying to filter the uncertainty from her voice.

"The job keeps me busy and in a small town, I need to be careful. If I date too many women, I'd quickly develop a reputation as a lady's man, like Chance before he settled down with Winter. It's simply easier not to date than to fish in a tiny pond," he said, lifting a shoulder in a shrug.

She bit her bottom lip. His gaze dropped to her mouth, and she wondered what his full lips would feel like pressed to hers. Not that she'd kissed many guys—she could count them on one hand and have fingers left over—but she was curious about *this* man.

Keeping her gaze locked on his, she propped her elbow on the table and leaned closer. "How long have you worked at Ironside Protection Services?"

The only light in the room came from the white twinkling lights wrapped around the Christmas tree, creating an intimate bubble in the dimly lit space between them.

"Three years."

Three years since his last relationship, give or take.

"What about you? No one special in your life?"

"There's no one. I never know when I might have to pick up and leave. Makes a relationship a complication I can't afford to have."

"People tend to describe relationships as complicated. This is the first time I've ever heard anyone refer to it as a complication."

Nora lowered her head and took a breath. "After my roommate, Jane, was murdered, I always worried that if I let anyone get close, I'd only be putting them in danger. So,

I never have." She looked around the room. "I didn't realize how late it had gotten."

The sun must have set hours ago, activating the automatic shades. Aside from the lit Christmas tree, the rest of the house was dark.

"Siri, turn on living room lights at sixty percent," he said. Soft amber lighting illuminated the space.

"Voice controlled smart lights. Nice. Can you do the same with the locks, thermostat and music?"

"Siri, play my work playlist—shuffled."

The smooth sound of jazz flowed from the speakers. "Coltrane?" she asked.

"Good ear," he said with a nod. "This is from his *My Favorite Things* album. You like jazz?"

"My stepdad loves it." The smile on her face faded. "At least he used to listen to it all the time. Now, I wouldn't know."

"Were you close to him?" he asked.

"Yeah, I was. Closer to him than my biological father. I called him Pa. My mom thought it was a nice compromise."

"Was a compromise necessary?"

She shrugged. "Mom used to say that my dad was a good guy. The memories I have of him are hazy. He stopped coming by to see me after he moved to Bull River, up in Canada. Mom said the divorce was hard for both of them, but he had difficulty watching her build a new family with Pa."

"How old were you when he relocated?"

"Not really sure. My sister, Rosa, was a toddler around that time. I guess I was about seven or eight." A rhythmic beeping sounded, the alert system warning a vehicle was headed toward his house.

"The pizza must be here."

"Does the alert go off as soon as someone turns down the road?"

"The wireless sensor has a quarter-mile transmission range, but I programmed it to go off once a car gets one hundred feet down the private road. The buffer gives someone a chance to make a U-turn in case they've taken a wrong turn before triggering the system."

Grabbing his phone with one hand, he got up from the table and rested his other hand on the hilt of the Glock holstered on his hip.

"I'm starving," she said. "Where are the plates?"

He started toward the front door. "Cabinet above the dishwasher."

A car door in the driveway closed.

"Bo," she said, drawing his attention. He stopped, looking back at her. "Thank you. For saying yes. For letting me stay here. It's nice not to be on the run again, alone in a hotel room, with only my thoughts to keep me company."

"You need help. We'll do everything in our power to protect you." Bo meant every word. Not only did Nora have him to rely on, but she also had the full force of IPS behind her. Although Chance was in Colorado, working on different IPS business for Rip Lockwood, he was only a phone call away. Autumn was busy analyzing the note cards that had been left for Nora and building out a profile of the killer. For years, Autumn had worked as a consulting forensic psychologist for the FBI before she burned out and sought a professional change in a location closer to her sisters. The other two guys, Eli and Tak, were going to begin updating the security system for a local business tomorrow, but if Bo needed them for an emergency, he could count on them to drop everything and be there.

"I appreciate it," Nora said.

Bo went up to the peephole and looked through it. Jeremy rounded the rear of his car and bound up the steps, carrying the food.

Taking his wallet from his back pocket, Bo fished out enough cash and opened the door.

Jeremy greeted him with a wide smile. "Evening. I made it here in twenty-four minutes."

"I hope you didn't have to speed to do it."

"Nope, I just made you my first stop."

Bo glanced over his shoulder while the kid tugged open the Velcro flap of the insulated bag. The driver's side door of his vehicle hung open. "Did you close one of the car doors? I thought I heard one shut."

Jeremy handed him the food and took the money. "Oh, that was probably the delivery guy."

Prickles crept up Bo's spine. "What delivery guy?" he asked, everything inside him tightening as he went on immediate alert. He looked around. Saw no one else.

The rhythmic beeps chimed. Bo whipped his phone out from his pocket.

"He was just here," Jeremy said. "A van was sitting on the main street like the driver was lost, but then he turned down your road right behind me."

Nora came up beside Bo.

He handed her the food. "Get back," he said, urging her away from the door. He brought up the security app, managing to catch a glimpse of the van leaving before it disappeared from sight.

"I assumed he was a delivery guy," Jeremy said, "because he hopped out with a package, dropped it off, and left before I even got out of the car." The young man bent down and picked up something nestled in the outer corner of the doorway. The kid handed him a red and gold box with a bow on top. "Here you go."

"Did you get a look at him?" Bo asked. "Did you see his face?"

"No. He had on a ball cap and hood. His head was down. I didn't think anything of it. Figured he was cold and in a rush. Why?"

Bo dropped the box on the floor and looked at Nora. "Get your gun and keep the door locked until I get back. Don't open it for anyone." He slammed the front door shut and hit a button on the keypad, locking it.

"Is something wrong?" Jeremy asked.

Without responding, Bo drew his gun, ran to his truck and fired it up. He sped down the private road, his heart slamming against his rib cage. Reaching the main street, he scanned the intersection in the hope of seeing which direction the van had gone.

No sign of the vehicle. He could've left either way. Both routes would eventually lead to the state highway.

Slamming his hand on the steering wheel, Bo swore. That monster had found her.

After they left IPS earlier, on the ride to his house, Bo had checked his mirrors to see if they were being followed, but truth be told, he hadn't been as vigilant as perhaps he should've. Had he been so distracted by her proximity in his truck that he'd missed a tail?

The killer had sat on the main road and waited for an opportunity to get close. To leave another package for her.

Nora.

Whatever was inside that box, he didn't want her to be alone with the contents.

Bo threw the truck in Drive, made a U-turn and rushed

back toward the house. Jeremy drove past, giving his horn a little honk and waved.

At the house, Bo screeched to a stop, dashed up the steps and inside to find Nora sitting still as stone at the table.

The red and gold box was open in front of her.

His mind raced with terrible possibilities of what might be in the box. He crossed the room, and the smell hit him first. The same cologne—smoky, spicy, a hint of sweetness. Reminded him of a campfire.

Tension crackled along his nerve endings like static on a dry day as he stepped up to the table. He looked over Nora's shoulder, down at the contents.

Another lump of coal. More sugar plums.

And another typed message on the same kind of card.

Denise Moore screamed and begged before she died.
Because you didn't play by the rules.
No police. No private investigators.
Go home. Alone. Or else.

Bo put the lid on the box, covering it. The note wasn't his most pressing concern. It was Nora. Sensing her vulnerability after what happened to her neighbor, he moved around the chair and crouched beside her. He gently took her trembling hands and held them. "Hey, look at me," he said, and her gaze lifted from the table to meet his. "You're not going back home and you're not going to be alone. Calling the police, going to IPS, was the right decision."

Her eyes turned glassy as she shook her head. "I got her killed."

"You are not responsible for what happened to your neighbor. You didn't take Mrs. Moore's life. That sick monster did. Don't let him saddle you with that kind of guilt because that's exactly what he wants. If you do, you'll react emotionally to this, and then you're as good as dead," he said, desperately needing her to believe him.

"It doesn't matter what I do. Where I go. He keeps finding me. Maybe I've been living on borrowed time and—"

"Nora," he managed to grind out and she stopped talking. "Santa Says, Sharks and Minnows—that's all a diversion. *This* is the real game. Getting you to give up. Getting you to make a mistake. Everything that you do matters. You have to keep fighting. You can't let him win."

She let out a shaky breath. "I want to see him behind bars or dead. But..." She tipped her head back and closed her eyes. "I don't want anyone else to get hurt because of me."

"You can't play his game. Do you understand?"

Sniffling, she nodded. "I refuse to let him win."

He was relieved to hear her say the words, but something in her voice didn't fully convince him.

The twisted animal stalking her had figured out Nora's weakness—her empathy. Her big heart and the way she cared about others, even for a neighbor. Like any weak spot, the killer was using it against her by applying pressure.

That perverse exploitation and the way she struggled not to cave to it reached out and grabbed hold of Bo. It gripped him where he was most vulnerable, making him long to comfort and protect her.

He put a palm on her cheek and caressed her face, and she looked down at him. He saw fear in her eyes, but determination, too. A resolve that had kept her alive thus far.

"I know that you've done this on your own for so long that it might be hard for you to trust IPS," he said. "To trust me. But you hired us, asked me to get personally invested, and now I am. You're not in this alone. Not anymore."

Tears tracked down her cheeks and she wrapped her

arms around his neck. On a reflex, he pulled her into a hug. Awareness infiltrated his veins as the smell of her hit him. Sugar cookies and sunshine—if sunshine had a scent that was what it'd be, light and warm and ethereal. The smell triggered a response deep inside him, one that he struggled to dismiss and, at the same time, ached to explore. He wanted a piece of that big heart of hers. Holding her close, with her face pressed to his throat, he wondered what it would be like. To have someone so brave and capable in his corner. Caring for him.

Maybe once the chaos subsided and they stopped the killer terrorizing her—and he wasn't her bodyguard anymore—he would ask her out on a proper date.

Maybe.

For now, his full focus had to be on protecting her. No room for anything else.

"Nora." Her name left his lips in a whisper. The killer wanted her isolated and afraid. Bo wasn't going to allow misplaced guilt to drive her to make a mistake that she'd regret. "Let me help you," he said.

"I will." She tightened her arms around him. "It's just that nothing ever works. Not for long. He just keeps coming after me."

Her breath brushed his cheek, warmth tickling his chilled face, and a shiver teased over every male nerve ending in his body.

The dampness from her tears soaked into the collar of his shirt and Bo held her tighter. He rubbed her back and gently squeezed her shoulder, doing his best to comfort her, to ease her trembling.

But she continued to shake and sob. He planted kisses on top of her head. "Shh. I'll get you through this." He kissed her brow and the corner of her eye, tasting her salty tears as he petted her hair. Trailed his lips lower, across her cheek.

Awareness buzzed through him. The need to console her slid toward something deeper, something more primitive. He eased back before he crossed a line, and they were nose to nose. His gaze fell to her mouth. Her rosy lips parted on a sigh, her breath hitching on a sob.

Her glassy eyes met his and then she looked down at his mouth.

Was she thinking the same thing as him?

If so, it made the thought doubly bad.

Clearing his throat, Bo started to stand, but Nora gripped his shirt collar, pulled him back down and pressed her lips to his.

Surprise jolted through him, pinning him to the spot, and he hesitated until her tongue penetrated the seam of his mouth. Electricity flared between them, and he kissed her back. Curling his fingers in her hair, he absorbed the feel of her soft curves moving against him. The heat of her mouth, the slip and slide of her tongue tangling with his, the warmth from her body seeping into him, seared him down to the bone.

Her hands roamed over him with a hunger that matched his. She tasted rich and sweet, fueling the desire burning in his veins. Lean muscle flexed beneath his palm, wicked curves molding to his hands as he explored her body.

Clinging to her, he lost himself in the moment. In her. In the way she sighed and how she excited him, rousing parts of him that had been dormant for far too long. He needed this kiss like a drowning man needed oxygen.

Her fingernails scraped against his scalp. "Bo."

The sound of his name pierced the bubble and it burst, bringing him back to his senses. What was he doing?

With a shuddering breath, he pulled back, dropping his hands to his sides. "I'm sorry. I don't know what I was thinking." That was the problem. He hadn't been thinking at all. Too caught up in the moment, feeling. "I shouldn't have done that."

She was upset. Distraught. Needed comfort.

Not to be pawed at and kissed and taken advantage of.

He should have consoled her. But only with his words. Nothing more.

Still, he wanted to kiss her again, with no holds barred.

She blinked up at him. Tears clung to her lashes, but she'd stopped crying. "Don't be sorry. I'm the one who kissed you."

True, but the problem was he had kissed her back.

"It wasn't professional," he said, stepping away from her. "It won't happen again."

But she eased closer, testing his restraint. "It's your job to help me, isn't it?"

"Yes, but..." Giving into his baser instincts wasn't what he wanted. His gaze dropped to her mouth again, and all sorts of dirty ideas sprang to mind. Ideas that would get him fired and get her hurt.

Hell. She was sexy and sensual and so soft. From the day he'd met her, he'd wanted her. And that made him the ultimate jerk because, at the time, she'd been shot and scared. Just as vulnerable then as she was right now.

He was the worst.

"A minute ago, I didn't need *professional* from you," she said. "I needed something more personal. A connection. To not *feel* alone." She swallowed as though it was hard for her to admit it. "You gave me that. To get through this, I might need more than a bodyguard. Maybe I need a friend, too."

Taking another step, erasing any space between them, she rested her head on his chest and leaned into him.

Steeling himself against the tempting feel of her body, he wrapped his arms around her, loosely, and steered his thoughts toward the job. The mission and nothing else. "We're going to find him," he said, thinking of the monster who had the audacity to leave that box on his doorstep, "and make him pay for what he's done."

No matter how long it took. Of that fact, he was one hundred percent certain.

How they would accomplish it, he had no idea. But he had to figure it out quickly. Something in his gut told him that from here on out, things were only going to escalate.

Chapter Six

The next day, three house tours had gone smoothly aside from the fact she didn't make a sale. The morning and lunch had been thankfully uneventful. Bo's diligence as a bodyguard should have put Nora at ease, but she was still on edge. Jumpy. Nerves raw.

She reminded herself it was to be expected. Somehow, she had managed not to think of Mrs. Moore or the threatening notes every single minute. Having Bo at her side helped. He was like a guardian angel, ready to shield her from any harm that might come their way. His protective instincts were sharp, and his unwavering commitment to keeping her safe gave her the confidence to face anything.

But in the back of her mind, it was like she was waiting for the guillotine to drop. Waiting for the killer to exact a new punishment for her defiance. Waiting for his next attempt on her life.

Emotions seesawed through her as Bo turned into the parking lot of the Methodist church that was situated between Bitterroot Falls and Cutthroat Creek. He drove around back and parked close to the auxiliary building where they ran the food pantry and soup kitchen.

She turned to him, wondering how they were going to handle things inside. "It was easy enough to pass you off as my assistant earlier while I was showing the houses, but that won't fly here." She nodded at the church's auxiliary building.

The pantry was open for three hours, three days a week, and once a month they served a hot meal. She donated her time whenever she was available.

A line had already started forming. The days when the church provided hot meals were the most popular. Not everyone who came was unhoused. Many were veterans or elderly, but all were in need, having a hard time making ends meet with the high cost of groceries.

"They know me and the real estate agency here," she said. "It's a small company. No one has an assistant." She certainly didn't want word of one to get back to her colleagues, stirring up professional trouble she didn't need. "Everyone will notice you hovering and you're not dressed like someone in need of a free meal. What should I tell people when they ask who you are?"

"Who do you want me to be?" he asked, his gaze searching her face.

A dangerous question that had her mind careening back to the hug he'd given her last night. To all the hugs since she'd learned of Mrs. Moore's murder. To the kiss they'd shared that had left her melting and aching for more.

She could take care of herself, but it was nice not to have to. Each time, his strong arms wrapped around her, it felt so good. Warm and comforting. It was an unexpected, pleasant change to have someone she could lean on.

Before one of Bo's embraces, she never would've thought a simple hug held the power to make a situation better. A little brighter. His strong yet gentle touch was a source of solace for her in the midst of this nightmare.

And kissing him transported her away from reality, made her want to forget the reason he was actually with her.

Because a relentless killer found me again.

Nora shrugged in response to his question. "I can't say you're a friend from out of town visiting me." Half the women in Bitterroot Falls had already noticed him strutting around. The other half found out who he was seven weeks ago. "The mass shooting made Ironside Protection Services a household name after you helped apprehend the sniper." The entire IPS team had been featured on the front page of the *Bitterroot Beacon*.

"Then there's two ways we can approach it. Option A, you could introduce me as your bodyguard. Explain that you've been harassed, threatened, and have a legitimate fear for your life."

Her stomach did a somersault at the suggestion and nausea swamped her. "I don't want to admit I have a bodyguard. There'd be too many questions. About me. My past. The looks of pity I'd draw." She shook her head as her chest tightened. Being in the spotlight was the last thing she wanted after years of learning how to navigate the shadows. "What's option B?"

"We tell them I'm your boyfriend," he said, and the knot in her chest loosened. "We say I've taken off a few days from work and I want to spend as much time with you as I can. But that would require us to act familiar with each other. Close. I'd have to touch you. Nothing to cross the line, just hold your hand or put an arm around you. Something like that."

A shiver trickled down her spine at the idea of him being her boyfriend. Faux boyfriend anyway. At having people believe it. But would they?

Licking her lips, she swallowed and looked away from him, suddenly worried about what he might see on her face.

She was always alone. Never dated. She hesitated at what to do.

"I think telling the truth is the way to go," he said, lightly. "It'll be awkward at first, but once folks get over their initial surprise, they'll be more apt to pay attention to anything suspicious, which is a good thing."

If they knew, they'd treat her differently. That would not be good for her. Half the day had been normal, or as close to it as possible. She wanted the remainder of the day to be the same. Was that too much to ask for? A bit of normalcy instead of nonstop turmoil?

The story was better than the truth and worth a try. "I don't want to tell them. Please."

"Well then, boyfriend it is."

Ignoring the sudden flare of heat in her cheeks, she nodded, suppressing a smile. "How long have we been dating in case they ask?"

"Keep it vague. Say it's new."

"Okay."

She tucked her purse under the passenger's seat. Sometimes drug addicts popped up for a hot meal and the director of the program, Susan Whitehall, advised them that it was best to leave any valuables locked in their vehicle.

They climbed out of his Tacoma. Bo came around to her side, took her hand in his, interlacing their fingers as they headed for the auxiliary building.

Big and brooding with a patient nature that calmed her and made her feel safe, Bo was the only one at IPS who she was willing to trust with her life. Having him pretend to be her boyfriend was a consolation prize for the fact that she needed protection.

"Do you think everyone has heard about Mrs. Moore?" she asked him. "I didn't see anything on the news about her this morning."

"Logan texted me that he was able to keep it quiet. Reporters haven't caught on yet. They will soon enough. But since the neighbors called it in, there's no way to know who they might've told. Just be prepared in case it comes up."

She nodded, bracing herself for anything.

Skirting the line, they went up to the door that had a sign stating the hours, and she knocked.

Susan glanced out through the glass panel at the top of the door and spotted her.

Nora smiled and waved.

The door swung open. Susan stepped out. "I was starting to get worried you wouldn't make it." The sixty-two-year-old woman gave her a one-armed hug and then gestured for them to enter. She turned to those standing in line. "Ten more minutes and we'll be ready for you all." Susan shut the door and faced the two of them. Her salt-and-pepper streaked hair was up in a bun. Reading glasses with a tortoiseshell frame hung from a braided leather strap around her neck. "I can always count on you, Nora, to keep the line moving. I don't know what I would've done without you. November and December are our busiest hot meal days." Susan looked at her companion. "Who do we have here?"

"This is Bo Lennox, my boyfriend," Nora said, without the last word sticking to the roof of her mouth.

Susan's face brightened with a wide smile. "Welcome, Bo. I recognize the surname as well as the face. You work over at that Ironside agency, don't you?"

"Yes, ma'am, Ironside Protection Services."

"If you call me ma'am, you'll make me feel my age. I'm Susan. We're a little short-staffed today. I could use you over in toiletries," she said, pointing to one end of the room. "Nora, you can work the food line as usual." Susan nodded to the opposite side, tables and chairs filled in the long space between.

"Today is my day off." Bo put his hand on Nora's lower back. "I was hoping to spend the day with her. Would you mind if we worked together?"

Susan smiled again, radiating warmth. "How sweet. I wish I had a handsome young man who couldn't keep his hands off me and wanted to spend the day at my side." She laughed, and they chuckled. "I can ask Roger to switch to toiletries, but he can be stubborn."

"Introduce me to him," Bo said, "and I'll take care of it."

Raising her eyebrows, Susan smirked. "You're welcome to try." She led the way over to the food line where everyone was setting up and introduced Bo to the group, saving Nora from doing it. "Roger, can you spare a minute?" Susan motioned for him to follow her off to the side.

Bo kissed Nora's cheek. "I don't think this will take long," he whispered.

"You don't know Roger," she responded in a low voice.

He winked and went to join Susan and Roger.

Nora watched him walk away and shake Roger's hand.

"I need to get shot," a woman said, and Nora jerked her gaze away from Bo's back—*and his very nice backside*—to see Kimberly setting down a pan of vegetables beside her.

"I'm sorry. What did you say?" Nora must've misheard her.

"You told me that a hot guy from IPS interviewed you after you were shot by the sniper. Remember? That's him, isn't it? You told me he gave you a ride home and everything." Kimberly waggled her eyebrows.

"There was no *everything* to the ride home. He was a perfect gentleman, and I didn't say he was hot." Even though he was hot enough to set every cell in her body ablaze.

Bo looked back at her and, to her surprise, gave her a discreet thumbs up. She smiled at him, her cheeks heating.

"You blushed when you spoke about him the way you're doing right now. Besides, all the guys at Ironside are yummy, aren't they?" Kimberly laughed and nudged Nora's arm with her elbow.

Everyone at IPS was smart, capable and undeniably attractive—including Autumn—but only Bo made her pulse quicken and her thighs tingle and her thoughts stray. Looking at him now, one word ran through her head on repeat. *Wow.*

"Good for you, finally getting a boyfriend and a handsome one to boot. You only had to take a bullet to do it."

"Is Carl here today?" Nora asked, mentioning Kimberly's husband.

The busty blonde-haired woman flattened her mouth in a tight line. "Yeah, he's over in toiletries." She waved a hand toward the far side of the room.

Grinning, Bo came back over. "It's done."

"How?" She lowered her voice. "He's the most resistant man."

"I disarmed him by starting off with the worst thing that might pop into his head. I told him he wasn't going to like what I had to say and even though he didn't know me, he was going to think I was a jerk. Then I simply asked him for a favor, explained the situation, apologized for the inconvenience and said that I'd be grateful."

"And that really worked?"

"Sort of. Roger likes you. Said how nice you are five times. I did have to promise to treat you right." He put his arm around her waist and kissed her cheek again.

Her face heated and she couldn't stop a smile from surfacing.

"She is the nicest," Kimberly said, reminding Nora of how close the woman was still standing. "Always volunteers to stay late for cleanup."

"It's a part of the job." Nora grabbed aprons, hairnets and gloves and handed Bo the things he needed to work the food line. "We all have to pitch in, even for the parts we might not enjoy."

Kimberly frowned. "Tell that to the ones who never help clean."

The comment was valid but pointing fingers never solved anything.

"I'm happy to pitch in and clean up," Bo said, "if I get to do it with my lovely girlfriend."

Another wave of heat suffused Nora's cheeks.

"Aww. I wish Carl said sweet stuff like that to me."

Susan clapped her hands, getting everyone's attention. "This is our last day to serve a hot meal for the rest of the year. Don't forget to smile and wish everyone a happy holiday. In two minutes, I'll start the music and let everyone in."

Nora couldn't help thinking about Mrs. Moore and how the sweet older woman wouldn't get to spend Christmas with her son and grandkids. Guilt didn't inundate her this time. Something Bo had told her last night clicked in her head.

Instead of allowing herself to feel guilty, she'd cling to her anger and her resolve and do the one thing the killer didn't want her to do. Survive.

Christmas carols played over the speakers and hungry people flowed inside, making her nerves flutter.

Yet, that little voice inside told her that as long as Bo was by her side, she'd be all right.

Chapter Seven

Bo smiled until his cheeks ached. "Happy holidays," he said with each serving of roast turkey he put on a plate. This was the third pan of meat that had been brought out from the kitchen.

Prior to today, he had no idea that there were so many people in need in the town and surrounding area. This wasn't a large city with unsheltered individuals living on the streets. But families and veterans and even college students who couldn't afford food filed into the building, thankful for the meal.

The food service was nearly finished and so far, so good. Keeping his head on a swivel, he scanned the room, memorizing faces, watching the crowd, scrutinizing any male around six feet tall with an average build. The killer could hide in plain sight here and they'd never know.

Bo had played back the video feed coverage from the front of his house when the pizza had been delivered. The man had anticipated a camera above the door and wore a scarf pulled up over his face and a nondescript ball cap with a hood, and he'd kept his head tilted down.

The killer had been on his doorstep, within his grasp, and yet, Bo wasn't any closer to identifying him.

No one had shown any aggression toward Nora at the

church. Though there'd been some attention that Bo had considered unwanted. One man kept looking at her like he was undressing her with his eyes and another asked her for extra bread rolls whenever there was a small break in the line.

"When are they going to let people have seconds if they're interested?" Bo asked her, though it was impossible to whisper amid the din of music and voices. Every table was full and engaged in lively conversations.

"Any minute now since things have slowed down. Less than a handful of new people have shown up during the past three songs."

He searched the crowd. "Where's that guy?"

"Which guy?" she asked, though he was certain she should know who he was talking about.

"The one who keeps asking for more rolls. He's too chatty. Complimenting you every time he comes over." Bo suspected he was on drugs. He had the classic signs of a methamphetamine user: shifty red eyes with dilated pupils, thinning hair, gaunt, decayed teeth and scabs on his face. He moved and spoke fast. Another guy with good, thick-soled work boots kept his distance at the far side of the room near toiletries and also gave Bo a bad vibe. At the moment, he couldn't spot either of them.

"He's only trying to get on my good side," Nora said, "so I give him extra bread. It doesn't mean anything."

"Everything means something."

The meth head emerged from the bathroom, and Bo watched the guy sit back down at a table near the food service line.

Bo's phone buzzed. Not a missed call or a text message. The vibration was constant, making his pulse spike. He dished out the serving of turkey he was holding onto the plate in front of him, set the tongs down and took out his cell phone.

"What is it?" She glanced at him as she spooned vegetables onto the person's plate and then added a bread roll. "Happy holidays," she said to the woman.

Bo looked down at the alert on his phone and tapped it. The steady vibration from his phone automatically stopped when the app opened, and he read the system message. "Someone's in the woods, approaching the house."

"Could it be an animal?"

"It's possible, but doubtful," he said, and alarm widened her eyes. The sensors had a fifty-foot-wide motion range and sometimes deer set them off, but he'd placed them well to reduce the probability. The real concern was the pattern of movement. "The first sensors triggered were near a road where someone would park and then enter the woods on foot. I can't see who or what it is. The cameras are positioned closer to the house. Right now, I only know there's movement."

Movement that had to be investigated.

"Do you need to leave?" she asked, as if picking up on what he was thinking. "Go out there and see who it is? If it's him?"

Bo didn't want to miss another opportunity to catch this guy, but he also couldn't leave Nora unprotected.

"No. I won't go, but I need to call the team. See if Tak and Eli can head out there." "Jingle Bells" boomed from the speakers. Kids ran around the space, playing and laughing. Mealtime chatter had grown even louder. "I'll step outside and give them a call."

It would also give him a chance to check for anyone suspiciously loitering outside the building. Movement at his house wasn't cause for him to lower his guard here at the church. This event was the perfect excuse for people to mill around with no questions asked.

"Okay," Nora said. "But if one of the guys can't investigate it, I understand if you need to leave. Everyone will be here for hours. We'll be serving food until seven and then we still have to clean up. I'll be fine if you need to go."

Bo wasn't willing to take that chance. "I'll be back in a few minutes." He leaned in and pressed a quick kiss on her forehead, his lips brushing against her warm skin. Only for the sake of maintaining appearances that they were a couple—at least that's what he told himself. But Bo found it hard to deny the faint flicker in his chest, the gentle spark that ignited between them every time he touched her.

Choosing option B had been a risky move because there was a glimmer of something real beneath the pretense. For him, anyway. He wondered whether it was the same for her.

If that kiss last night was any indication that she was interested in him and hadn't simply been in need of affection, the comfort of any bodyguard, then he had his answer.

Dismissing the rogue thought, he made a beeline for the door and brought up his list of favorites on his phone. He hit Tak's name first.

"We have enough food left," Susan said, "to invite those still hungry to come up for a second helping. We ask that you allow expectant mothers and children to go to the front."

People got up and started forming a line again.

A commotion at the other end of the room had Susan rushing to the far side, where toiletries were handed out.

The guy Bo had mentioned jumped up out of his seat and hustled over to her. "Can I just take four rolls? I'll leave the meat for the others. Please, pretty lady. Those keep and I can munch on them for a couple of days."

Sighing, Nora looked at the kids moving through the line toward her and then down at the aluminum pan. There were only six rolls left. "Go ahead and take the rest."

"You're an angel." Beaming, the guy scooped up the remainder of the bread. "Thank you so much."

She turned to Kimberly. "Cover the turkey and veggies. I'm going to run to the kitchen to grab some more bread rolls. Tell whoever wants any more to hang here until I get them. It'll only take a sec."

Kimberly nodded. "Sure thing."

Nora grabbed the pan and hurried off through the double doors into the kitchen. Glancing around, she spotted the bags of bread lined up on a long, stainless-steel table in the rear of the room. She headed to the back part of the kitchen, set the pan down and started opening the rolls.

Dumping the last bag of bread that would fit in the pan, she sensed a presence right before she heard the footsteps drawing close, the soft thud of thick rubber soles on the linoleum floor.

She turned and took a step back, a gasp stuck in her throat. Alarm crawled up her spine.

A man glared down at her. His eyes were barely visible, his features distorted through a nylon stocking covering his face.

Her pulse skyrocketed when she tried to run. But he was already too close and lunged at her.

He threw her into the stainless steel table, dazing her. A tremendous weight slammed onto her, his chest bearing down on her back. His arm coiled around her throat, putting her in a chokehold, cutting off her windpipe.

Panic raced over her like a thousand fire ants, stinging her skin.

"Get rid of him," he growled in her ear.

Without thinking, she clawed at his forearm, trying to dig her nails into his flesh, but the padding of his coat was too thick to do any damage. Her reflexes were slow and sticky as glue.

"Get rid of him and go home alone. Understand?"

Her vision blurred, her head starting to swim as she battled for oxygen. Dark spots flashed in her eyes. She flailed, hitting his arm, scratching his face, trying to get free, but felt like she was sinking, going under.

Six seconds. That's all she had. Maybe eight and she would lose consciousness. She had to do something.

"If you don't," he said, his breath foul, "more will die. More minnows will bleed."

The last words sliced through the paralyzing haze clouding her mind. Panic receded, like the tide ebbing, and all her training flowed back into her. She put her foot up on the table and used it as leverage, pushing away from it as he repeated the same warning.

"Get rid of—" The force cut him off, and he reared back from the table, dragging her with him.

The move created a pocket of space between her chin and his elbow. Wedging her fingers into the gap, she tucked her head, relieving the pressure on her throat. She could breathe.

Muscle memory kicked in, spurring her into action.

With a sudden burst of adrenaline, she dropped one hand from his arm, twisted her torso and thrust her elbow back hard into his belly.

A shocked grunt whooshed from his lips, and he released his grip on her.

She raised her forearm, keeping her elbow bent parallel to her chest, and rotated her entire body, generating as much momentum as possible as she spun on her heel and struck his head with her arm.

He wobbled backward, knocked off balance.

A deep ache flared in her bad shoulder, but she ignored the pain and sucked in a breath. Seizing the opportunity, she rammed the hard, meaty part of her palm up into his nose. A sickening crunch of bone and snap of cartilage filled the air, and he cried out in pain. She drove her boot heel into his groin, shoving him away from her.

The man doubled over in agony and reached out for the counter, steadying himself. Swearing and calling her foul names, he grabbed something. Metal glinted in his hand. A knife.

A surge of dread spiraled through her, spilling into her mouth bitter as bile. She backed away. Spun for the double doors and ran. For help. For safety.

Fueled by desperation, she cried out.

The man's vulgar insults and profanities barely registered in her ears over the pounding of her heart and her own shrill voice.

Screaming, she shoved through the doors and out of the kitchen and barreled into a wall of solid muscle.

"Nora!" Bo's arms closed around her. "Are you all right?" His frenzied hands raked over her. "What happened? Are you hurt?"

She shook her head. Nausea robbed her of the words. She fought to find her voice and snuff out the panic and fear flaring through her as hot and uncontrollable as wildfire.

"It's him," she panted. Everything hit her in a wave, bowling her over, and she crumpled to her knees. "He attacked me. In the kitchen."

Others rushed to her side. Bo leaned Nora against Kimberly, who held her, and he took off, disappearing through the double doors.

Shaking, Nora squeezed her eyes shut, taking deep breaths, trying not to throw up.

"You're going to be okay," Kimberly said as Nora faintly heard someone on the phone with 911. "Oh, my God. You're bleeding." Kimberly held up her bloody sleeve. "Were you cut, honey?" The blonde inspected her arm.

"No." The word squeaked out of Nora. She tried to remember exactly what happened, and it was like pressing down on an open wound. The man had gotten a knife, but he hadn't cut her. "I don't think so." She'd thrown a palm-heel strike to his face. "I think it's his blood." From when she broke his nose.

She couldn't stop shaking.

Safe. She was safe.

A small crowd had gathered around her. She would be all right.

Seconds passed—maybe minutes—before Bo reappeared, pushing through the kitchen doors. He cut through the bodies, parting the crowd, and rushed to her, sinking to his knees beside her.

He pulled her into his arms and held her close. "He got away. Through the back door. Ran to his car. I got a make and model, but only a partial license plate." Rocking her gently, he kissed her forehead and stroked her hair. "Shh. We'll get him. Don't cry. I've got you." More kisses. "Please, don't cry."

That's when it hit her: she was sobbing.

She struggled to get a grip, to regain control. She sank into his embrace and strained to draw on his strength, but all she could do was clutch Bo tighter as tears continued to fall.

Chapter Eight

Staring at Nora as a doctor treated her in the Cutthroat Creek Community Hospital emergency room, Bo stood in terrified shock. His heart had been lodged in his throat since she was attacked at the church.

Bo slipped up, and it stung. But what he felt meant nothing. Nora was terrified and in pain. Only she mattered.

"You're not seriously injured. But I don't like the bruising on your throat," the ER doctor said as he examined her neck. He traced the line of her old scar with a gloved finger. "This isn't the first time that you've been attacked."

"No," she said, her voice raspy. "It's not."

But it was the first time that monster had gotten close enough to touch her since she'd hired IPS, and he was supposed to be protecting her.

He'd left her alone for a short time. *Ten minutes. Less. Surrounded by people.*

People who didn't know they needed to look out for her. Who were unaware that she was in danger.

Because they'd chosen to go with option B—a lie.

A lie he'd gotten wrapped up in, playing the part of her boyfriend when his sole focus should've been on his role as bodyguard.

A lie that endangered her.

The mistake was his and the blame for the harrowing ordeal she'd barely survived rested squarely on his shoulders. He allowed her to carry on as if nothing was wrong, business as usual, hoping to lure the killer out. And it had worked. They had baited the devil himself.

Bo never should have left her side. Not for a single minute. He swore beneath his breath.

"Will I have to be admitted?" Nora asked. "Or am I okay to leave?"

"Your throat is going to be sore for a few days. Ice the bruises. I'll get your discharge paperwork started and write a prescription for painkillers."

"You can skip the prescription," she said. "I won't take anything that'll make me drowsy."

Of course not. She needed to be alert and ready for anything, especially with Bo as her bodyguard. He clenched his jaw.

"If you say so, but you should take an over-the-counter anti-inflammatory." The doctor jotted something down on a clipboard. "We'll get you out of here in a little bit."

At the sound of footsteps, Bo looked over to his right and spotted Logan at the nurse's station along with Tak and a female officer in uniform, who was most likely there to collect any forensic evidence.

The nurse pointed to the bay Nora was in. Their gazes found him, and Logan motioned for Bo to come over.

Bo gave a single nod to him and looked at Nora. "Logan and Tak are here. I need to talk to them while an officer collects any possible physical evidence. She'll inspect under your fingernails and most likely clip them. Maybe you scratched him and have his DNA."

"You're leaving me again?" she asked, her eyes wide, her voice hoarse.

His heart sank.

The doctor glanced between them. "I'll give you two a moment," he said, then stepped out of the bay.

"No. I'm not going anywhere." Bo found himself needing to soothe her, to alleviate the anxiety he'd caused with his negligence. "I'm sorry I left you. For what happened." *On my watch.* He eased closer and took her hand. "I'll be at the nurse's station, just a hundred feet away, where I can keep an eye on anyone coming in and out of this cubicle." He wouldn't so much as go to the bathroom or grab a cup of coffee. Not unless Tak or Logan was within arm's reach of her. "I promise," he said, giving her hand a reassuring squeeze.

She hesitated and then nodded.

As he stepped out, the female officer entered the bay, carrying an evidence kit.

"Hello, Ms. Santana. I'm Officer Midthunder. I'll collect any possible DNA from the perpetrator."

"His blood is on her sleeve," Bo said, wanting to make sure it wasn't missed.

"Thank you. I'll go over everything with Ms. Santana," Officer Midthunder said and pulled the curtain closed.

Bo headed to the nurse's station.

"How is she doing?" Tak asked as Bo approached them.

"No serious injuries." Bo stood in between them with his back to the desk so that he could see the curtained cubicle Nora was in. "But the doctor doesn't like the bruises on her throat." Neither did Bo. He gritted his teeth at the pain she was in.

"I'm sorry to hear about what happened," Logan said. "I put out an APB on the car."

A black Subaru Outback. There were so many of those in the area that it might as well have been one of the unofficial state vehicles, second only to a Ford F-150. "But since you only have a partial plate, the odds are low that you'll find it. Right?"

Logan sighed. "A partial is better than nothing. Unfortunately, we didn't get anything helpful on CCTV. Not much coverage around the church."

Bo swore, his frustration wrestling with his anger. The only thing that was stronger was the guilt welling behind his sternum. This guy put his hands on Nora—hurt her, nearly choked her to death—and somehow managed to slip through Bo's fingers again.

"I questioned the folks who were still at the church," Logan said, taking out his notepad. "Turns out a tweaker saw the most." He thumbed through the notes. "Ricky Rooney is his name. Rooney knew Nora was going to the kitchen to refill the pan with bread rolls and watched her, hoping to snag some more before he left. Rooney saw a guy lurking in a corner. White man with a goatee, average height, average build. Dark eyes. Black hair. Broncos ball cap. Rooney claims the man crept toward the kitchen in a hurried manner. That he looked 'sus.' The man shoved his cap in his pocket as he took something else out. Whatever it was, Rooney stated the man pulled it over his head when he slipped into the kitchen."

Bo clenched his hands into fists. "The guy with the good work boots." The ache in his chest began to give way to a burning fury. "I spotted him, but he kept his distance. Stayed at the far side of the room with his head down. I thought he might've left when I stepped outside to call Tak because I didn't see him hanging around anymore," he said, his gut burning. "Why didn't Rooney tell someone about this guy after he saw him following Nora into the kitchen?"

Logan shrugged. "Rooney is an addict. Drawing attention to trouble isn't second nature to a guy like him. In fact, his survival instincts probably told him to look the other way. We're fortunate he gave us a statement at all. He said that Nora was so nice to him—the only one to let him have so many bread rolls—that he felt bad for her. I did find the ball cap at the scene, and I'll have it processed at the lab."

"Has Rooney ever seen the man with the goatee before? Maybe at the church?" Tak asked. "Is he a regular?"

"Nope." Logan shook his head. "Never seen him before. Rooney said the guy didn't eat. Only got toiletries and kept to himself."

Bo lowered his head, wishing he had handled things differently. "I knew the guy with the goatee was trouble." Precisely what kind, he hadn't been sure.

The guy who had dropped off the package at his house wore a plain black ball cap and moved differently. There was a slickness to him. Better stealth. Whether or not he had facial hair, Bo couldn't say because of the scarf over his face. Mr. Goatee with the work boots struck him as a criminal. A petty thief. Someone who snatched purses, stole cars, broke into someone's house while they were on vacation.

Not a cold-blooded killer with the patience to stalk someone for a decade.

How could Bo have gotten it so wrong? Why didn't he haul the guy outside and interrogate him, even if it was only based on a vibe? He could have dealt with any questions from the church staff and complaints from the guy later.

"I should've taken an aggressive, not-so-subtle approach with him," Bo said. "Then Nora wouldn't have been attacked."

"Beating yourself up over it isn't going to help Nora," Tak said. "Besides, now we have something to go on. If we have his blood, we've got his DNA. Plus a make and model of his vehicle. That puts us a lot closer to catching him than we were before."

"He's right." Logan nodded in agreement. "If you had scared him off before he had a chance to act, we'd never know who we were looking for. As unfortunate as the circumstances are, this helps."

The two men were his friends, his family. They were going to support him in this. Bo wished Eli was here. They were close as well, but E didn't care if he hurt someone's feelings. Not if they had messed up and needed a dose of harsh truth to get their act together.

"I need to get her statement," Logan said. "Officer Midthunder should be wrapping up."

Bo led the way toward the curtained cubicle.

A nurse he recognized entered the corridor. Kimi. She was the younger sister of Jacy, a combat engineer they'd served with who had died on a deployment. Jacy and Tak had been best friends.

"Hey, Kimi," Bo said when she stopped in front of them.

"What are you guys doing here?" Kimi glanced at the group. "Is everyone okay?" Her gaze landed on Tak, but he didn't respond.

"We're fine," Bo said, and a look of relief washed over Kimi's face. "It's a long story, but an IPS client was attacked. She's going to be okay. The doctor says she can be discharged soon."

"Glad to hear she's all right." Kimi folded her arms, her expression turning uneasy as her gaze shifted. "Takoda, do you have a minute to talk in private?"

Tak shook his head. "I'm working," he muttered and gestured to Bo that they should move on.

The tension was palpable. Bo had never seen Tak be cold

to anyone, much less Kimi, but Bo had his own problems to deal with.

"Bad timing. We're really busy," Bo said. "We'll catch up soon." He gave Kimi a quick hug and proceeded to Nora's cubicle. "Knock, knock. Is it okay for Logan to get your statement now?"

Officer Midthunder pulled back the curtain. "We're all done in here." The cop closed the kit and removed her latex gloves. "Ms. Santana got the guy good. His blood and skin were under her nails. Based on what she described during the altercation, I think she might have broken his nose."

"Not 'might,'" Nora said. "I did."

Tak smiled at her. "Good for you."

Officer Midthunder grabbed her kit. "I'll get out of your way so you can get your statement, Detective," she said and left.

"Nora, you never should've been in that position—where you had to defend yourself," Bo said, looking at her. "I should have been inside the building next to you the entire time." He took a breath, steadying himself for the next thing he had to say. "If you don't want me on your case anymore and would prefer to be reassigned to someone else at Ironside, no one would blame you." Tak and Eli had tactical training. The same as him. Any one of them would be a suitable replacement.

To his surprise, he now hated the idea. Deep down, he no longer wanted anyone to replace him.

Bo wanted to be the one to protect Nora. Which was ludicrous. But it was also as real as his feelings for her. He didn't want to leave her or let her down.

He only wanted to make good on his promises to her.

Nora narrowed her eyes at him, giving him a dirty look. "You didn't want to be my bodyguard from the beginning.

If you want to use what happened at the church as an excuse to have someone else assigned to me, then just say so. But don't turn it around on me because I have not lost faith in you," she said, and he was humbled by her confidence in him. "It's not too late for me run again if you want to wash your hands of me."

Bo met her fiery gaze evenly and gave her a steady nod. "No. I want you, Nora." The words effortlessly slipped out of his mouth, and her face softened. Then he realized what he'd said. "To stay with me. As my assignment." He shook his head. "I mean client." Nothing sounded right.

A tentative smile tugged at the corners of her mouth.

Tak put a hand on Bo's shoulder. "I think we've settled that and don't need to say anything else on the matter."

Bo was grateful to his friend, the man who was as close to him as a brother, for the change in the subject as well as for the way Nora was looking at him now. With a soft smile and a gleam in her eyes.

Logan pulled out a pen. "Walk me through what happened, Nora."

She sat straighter, looking poised, almost as if nothing had happened at all. But the path of recent tears stained her cheeks, her left hand trembled ever so slightly and there was no ignoring the nasty bruises on her neck. She wasn't as composed as she appeared, but she was doing a good job faking it. Bo respected the hell out of her effort after what she'd endured.

"We were on the line, serving food, when Bo got an alert on his phone that there was movement on his property," she said. "It was noisy inside with the music playing and everyone talking, so Bo went outside to call someone on his team to go to his place and check it out. We ran out of bread rolls and one guy really wanted more. I would've asked Susan to grab them, but something happened on the opposite side of the room—some kind of commotion that she needed to attend to. So I went to the kitchen to get them. I've done it before. Plenty of times. It usually only takes a couple of minutes."

One vulnerable minute, sixty seconds, was all that animal had needed to get to her.

Nora took a deep breath like she was forcing herself to continue and Bo wanted her to get through it as quickly as possible.

"He snuck up on me. By the time I realized he was there, it was too late."

"Did you get a look at him?" Logan asked.

"Briefly. Dark hair. Dark eyes. Facial hair."

Logan nodded. "Do you think a forensic sketch artist could help you recreate what he looks like?"

"No. He wore panty hose over his head. It distorted his face. His features were all mushed against the nylon."

"About how much did he weigh?"

She shrugged. "Maybe a little less than Bo."

"Two hundred." Bo had sized the guy up and estimated he weighed about ten to fifteen pounds less than he did.

Logan wrote it down. "He surprised you. Then what happened?"

"He grabbed me around the throat. Got me in a rear chokehold. But I fought him off."

"I'm sure the incident must've been terrifying," Logan said, sympathy heavy in his tone. "If he caught you by surprise and overpowered you, sounds like you got lucky to fend him off."

"I got lucky when I was sixteen and a couple of guys stopped him from getting me into a van. I got lucky when my roommate came back to the dorm early and he killed her instead of me. This time, it wasn't luck. I've trained for years in self-defense and martial arts so that when he attacked me again, I would be prepared." Her fingers curled around the sheet covering the lower half of her body and she looked down. "But I was petrified. At first, I froze. My mind blanked." She put a hand on her throat that was red and bruised and would be purple tomorrow. "I responded instinctively until my training finally came back to me. Muscle memory kicked in and I kicked his butt."

Bo wrapped an arm around her and rubbed her shoulder. "That was brave of you. To fight through the fear. Not everyone can."

She flicked a glance at him and offered a small smile, but it didn't last. "When he grabbed a knife, I saw a chance to get out of there and took it. I ran."

"Did he say anything to you?" Bo asked.

"Actually, he did. He warned me to get rid of you. Get rid of you and go home alone. Or more will die. More minnows will bleed."

"He referred to me, specifically? Not IPS like he did in the note card last night?"

"Yes. *Get rid of him*. That's what he demanded."

"Back up." Logan put a hand on his hip. "What note card last night?"

Bo quickly explained about the box that had been delivered. He'd updated the team, ensuring Autumn received pictures of everything, but he should've looped Logan in as well.

"Anything else you've forgotten to tell me?" Logan asked.

Bo shook his head and looked at Nora. "Did he use a voice modulator? You told us that every time you've had any interaction with him, even over the phone, he used a digital voice modifier."

She thought for a moment. "No," she said. "But he kept his voice low, kind of raspy. It made me think of a geriatric smoker, like he was trying to force it to sound different from his normal voice. I don't know. Maybe I'm reading too much into it."

"Did you smell anything?" Bo asked. "The same cologne from the note cards?"

She shook her head. "He reeked of cigarettes. The smell was on his clothes and his breath when he warned me. Then he dragged me backward. I went on autopilot, I guess. Fought back, got away from him and ran from the kitchen."

Once Bo walked back inside the building and he saw Nora missing from the food line, it was as if the devil had crawled out of hell and ripped his heart out of his chest. He asked Kimberly where she went and rushed to the kitchen.

"At that point, I came back inside," Bo said. "I realized what happened and ran after the guy through the back door of the kitchen. But he got away."

"Was anyone able to check out the sensors at your house?" Nora asked.

Excellent question. "Did you find out who was at my place?" he asked Tak.

His buddy shook his head. "No. I walked through the quadrant you identified from the triggered sensors. There were fresh tracks. Human. And white-tailed deer, too. Looked like someone was hunting. Whoever it was made a kill and dragged the animal back to his vehicle. A couple of shots hit some trees. Took out one sensor. Could've been an accident."

Everything about this situation rubbed Bo wrong. "Maybe."

"It's pretty late in the season for hunting," Logan said.

"Unless you're using a muzzleloader. Did you see any evidence that he was?"

Tak shrugged. "Can't say for sure. The hunter dug out the ammo that hit the tree and knocked out the sensor. But I replaced it with a camera for you and made sure it was working properly on your security system."

Both Tak and Eli had access to his place in case of an emergency, and he had access to theirs. "Appreciate it."

"What's a muzzleloader?" Nora looked between them. "And what difference does it make?"

"A muzzleloader is any firearm where the user has to load the projectile and the propellant charge into the muzzle end of the gun," Bo explained. "During the general season, which ended in November, regular rifle hunters have a huge advantage over muzzleloaders—just like archery—so they have their own season. Which is now."

"Do you usually get a lot of hunters out there?" Logan asked.

"When I bought the place, the previous owner told me it was a great hunting spot and he allowed others to use the land. I painted a purple stripe on trees along the perimeter of the property line to let folks know they're trespassing, but on occasion, a hunter will follow prey past the line. In an effort to be a friendly neighbor, I always let it slide. It wasn't a big deal." Then again, he'd never used his place as a safe house before either. Now any trespassing was a serious issue. "That's why I don't normally keep my security system active."

"Well, muzzleloader season will be over soon." Logan glanced at his phone. "In fact, today is the last day. Starting tomorrow, anyone hunting, even with a license or a muzzleloader, is breaking the law. That's in addition to trespassing. Any activity on your land should stop."

Tak slid a furtive glance at him. The question in his eyes was evident.

What if the activity in the woods didn't stop?

Then that meant it wasn't a coincidence and Bo's problem was about to get a whole lot more complicated.

Tak nodded as if reading his mind. "You need me, I'm there. E, too."

With a phone call, Tak could be on the west side of his property in ten minutes. Eli to the north in fifteen. "Yeah, I know. Thanks."

The monster stalking Nora wasn't just dealing with Bo. The entire IPS team would be there for her.

Chapter Nine

Sated, but not filled to excess, Nora set her chopsticks down on her plate. She'd showered and changed into a T-shirt and sweats as soon as they got back to the safe house.

"Did it hit the spot?" Bo asked her, packing up the leftovers.

"Dinner was good." Eating late was something she generally avoided, but it was either that or not eat, yet again. She skipped dinner last night after the red and gold box had been delivered. Tonight, between the incident at the church and the trip to the hospital and the police report, they didn't get back to Bo's house until nine. "I've never eaten at the Golden Dragon." She grabbed both their plates and took them to the sink. "When I'm in the mood for Asian food, I always go to the Ramen House for some reason."

"It's because you're loyal." He came up alongside her, taking the dishes from her hands.

"Oh, you think so?"

"Yep. I bet you know the name of the owner, who probably gives you a discount and allows you to leave your business cards for patrons to take because you're so loyal."

Mr. and Mrs. Yee were a sweet couple. They always gave her a free order of soup instead of a discount and did let her leave her business cards.

Grimacing, she shook her head. "Am I really that easy to read?"

"Not at all." He started washing the plates. "I just pay attention to the things you say, the way you speak about people. Take me for example. After what happened to you this evening at the church, you should've kicked me to the curb and insisted on a new bodyguard," he said, almost sounding annoyed with her for not having done so.

Pursing her lips, she grabbed a dish towel and dried the first plate. "That wasn't your fault." She set the dish on the rack.

"Like hell it wasn't." He handed her the second one.

As she took it, their fingers grazed. Electric heat zipped through her. Their gazes met and held. And held. And held. Her breath caught in her throat and she tried to ignore the spike of heat that was spiraling through her body.

He looked away and lowered his hand.

She dried the dish, set it down and turned toward him. "You didn't leave me. You stepped outside to make an urgent phone call. It was hard enough to hear yourself think in there with the music and everyone talking and the kids running around." She expected no less. It was the holidays after all. Even though she dreaded this time of year, the staff who organized the food pantry didn't want folks in need to dread it. They wanted hungry people to enjoy a hot meal and not to worry about where the next one was going to come from for an hour. She helped give them that. "We needed you to be discreet. Remember? You, yelling on the phone, not able to hear the person on the other end, would have defeated that goal."

"For all the good it did."

She put a hand on his chest and it was like touching a

flame. She soaked in the heat of him, wanting to steal some of it, wanting him to warm every cell in her body.

"The truth is that I shouldn't have gone to the kitchen alone." She'd done it a hundred times. Didn't think twice about it. But today was different and she should've acted accordingly. "I could've asked Kimberly to grab extra rolls. Or I could've waited until Susan was free again. You expected me to stay on the line, surrounded by people, and I didn't. I made a mistake." And paid the price. "You know what they say about hindsight being twenty-twenty."

He caressed her face. "Nora—"

"Bo," she cut him off with that firm tone he liked to use on her. It worked, too, though his gaze was fixed on her neck. On her bruises. "I'm not giving up on you and you're not getting rid of me that easily." Moving her hand from his chest, she tugged on her collar, wishing she was wearing something with a higher one, then playfully punched his arm. "Got it?"

"Yes, ma'am."

"I don't want to think about it more." When he called her ma'am, it reminded her that she was the client, which meant she was in charge. Sort of. "Right now, your job is to distract me."

He sighed. "Do you want to play cards?"

"Sure. Gin rummy?"

Nodding, he led the way into the living room where he had already built a fire. He grabbed a deck of cards from inside a side table. "Siri, play Christmas music."

"Deck the Halls" started.

She groaned and sat beside him.

"Not a fan of the artist or genre?" he asked, shuffling the cards.

"The entire season. The Yuletide Killer ruined it for me."

"Siri, stop." He frowned. "I should've anticipated that. It makes sense, considering. I'm sorry."

"You're not a mind reader. No need to apologize."

"What kind of music do you listen to? And don't tell me 'anything.'"

She smiled. That was going to be her answer. Surviving meant getting along with others. Not standing out or making waves. Blend in to stay alive. "Country and alternative rock."

"Alternative rock can vary quite a bit. Name three of your favorite bands."

"U2, Imagine Dragons and Muse."

"A woman after my own heart. Siri, play Alternative Soul playlist."

An artist she didn't recognize came on, but she liked it. "Who is this?"

"AWOLNATION. If anything pops up that you don't care for, just let me know." He offered her the cards. "Hey, I was wondering, after your biological father moved to Canada, you never saw him again?"

Shaking her head, she cut and handed the cards back. "He agreed to sign the paperwork for Pa to adopt me and I heard he later remarried. Had another kid. Moved on like my mom did, I guess."

"You were never curious about him?"

"He bailed on me. Frank essentially raised me. I'm the woman I am today because of him and my mom, right?" And also because of that sick man who killed her friends. He forced her to become strong, to learn how to fight to survive. "Since my dad chose to leave me, I guess there was always something… Not missing, but this other side to things, I suppose. It's hard to explain. I'm grateful to Frank, for stepping in and being a dependable father figure for me."

"You were fortunate to have that."

Not everyone did. Like Bo. "I've been meaning to ask you something."

"What's that?" he asked, passing out the cards.

"Is 'Bo' short for something?"

He stopped dealing. For the longest moment, he said nothing, holding the cards, and when his gaze finally lifted to hers, his expression was shuttered. "Yes. It's short for Boaz."

Boaz. Strong. Unique. Like him. "That's from the bible, isn't it?"

"The name is in the bible, but I don't know if that's the reason it was given to me. Maybe it was a family name and there's no religious meaning to it." His broad shoulders shrugged like it meant nothing.

But she could tell that it meant quite a lot.

Nora put her hand on his forearm. "We don't have to talk about it. I only ask because I want to get to know you better."

"I wish I knew more so that I could tell you. About my childhood. My family. My mother."

"How old were you when you were put into foster care?"

"Six."

So very young. "Do you remember her, your mother?"

"Bits and pieces. I remember her bathing me. Singing to me. Making me laugh. I never had a lot of toys. But there were a ton of books. And crayons. She read to me a lot and always asked me to draw her a picture."

Running her hand over his arm, she pressed her cheek to his shoulder. Subtle traces of soap clung to his skin, citrus and cedar, mingled with the warm scent of a man.

"With a library card, books are free," she said, "unlike toys. Sounds like she loved you. A lot."

"Yeah. Maybe," he said, his voice dismissive. "I like to think so." His swallow was audible. "But then a little voice reminds me that she didn't love me enough. I wasn't enough to get her to stay clean and sober. I wasn't worth fighting for. Worth living for."

Nora wanted to ask more about his mother and the situation. Instead, she held her tongue and let him continue when he was ready. She kissed his shoulder and stroked his hair. Several minutes passed in silence with her touching him.

What he shared was heavy. What if he thought she wasn't strong enough to hear it, to carry his truth?

"Your dad?" she asked. Two words, telling him she wanted to know more if he was willing to share it with her.

"According to my file, my mom was a single parent with no other living relatives. She struggled to stay away from alcohol and drugs. It's the reason I'm not a big drinker. Two beers. That's my max."

She hadn't seen any alcohol in the house and not even beer in the fridge. "Did a social worker get involved somehow when you were little?"

"Yes. Someone reported an illegal daycare operating from an apartment in our building."

"Where was this?" She had no idea where he grew up.

"Back in Denver. Social services looked into the situation and investigated the parents of all the children. The case worker, Tania Burgess, gave my mom opportunities to make changes." He shrugged. "Ms. Burgess finally deemed my mom unfit to provide a safe and nurturing environment. I went into the foster care system. I was constantly transitioning, bouncing from home to home. Some of the families I was placed with were kindhearted people. Unfortunately, not all foster parents had the same dedication. For some, fostering was merely a means to collect a check. I was trapped until I aged out of the system when I turned eighteen. By then, my mother was dead. Leaving me alone with so many unanswered questions."

The gravity of that hit her right in the chest, making her hurt for him. She'd been robbed of so much of her life because she had to run, hide and avoid any emotional entanglements, knowing she might have to disappear at any moment.

He'd been robbed, too. Of his past. Of his history. Of knowing where he came from. But at least he'd found a place where he belonged.

She stole a glance at his face.

His eyes were cast down at the table. He sat on the sofa's edge now, his knees spread wide, leaning forward, with his elbows resting on his thighs.

Nora ached to touch him, more than his forearm or his hair. To comfort him, the way he had for her. "Addiction can be hard." Putting a hand on his back, she spread her fingers wide and rubbed him gently. Curled her other hand around his arm. Pressed her cheek to his shoulder. "The way it destroys a person, their life, the lives of those closest. Especially if they don't have a support system, which it sounds like your mom didn't have," she said softly. "Her struggle had nothing to do with you. It didn't mean she didn't love you. Didn't mean you weren't worthy. The baths, the books, the singing and the laughter—those good memories meant she tried because she cherished you."

He didn't pull away from her. Didn't react. Not for several heartbeats, until he covered her hand—which gripped his arm—with his own and tilted his head so their foreheads touched.

"Have you ever thought about doing one of those genealogical tests, to track down other relatives?" she asked, wondering if she was a horrible person for pushing this.

"No. I don't trust the companies. There are too many

lawsuits against them for not properly disclosing what they do with your data. And what happens to your DNA when one of those companies goes out of business? Even if your genetic data isn't sold, it can always be stolen by hackers. I'm too paranoid."

Keeping up the caress on his back, she angled toward him and brushed her lips on his brow. Slowly, she felt his muscles relax beneath her touch. "What about contacting the social worker who handled your case? Maybe she remembers something that wasn't in the file you read."

"That was so long ago. I doubt she'd remember me or my mom out of thousands of cases. We're talking twenty-seven years since then."

Longer than she'd been alive, but the timeline nailed down his age to thirty-three as she'd guessed. "I wish you got closure or at least some answers."

"I have these vague, disjointed, happy memories of my mother. But they're all tied up with sadness. And loss. Like..." His voice trailed off.

She ran her fingers over his hair and guided his head to her shoulder. Lying back against the sofa, putting her head on the arm, she eased him down with her and wrapped her arms around him.

To her surprise, he let her.

"Like what?" she asked softly.

"Like there's a hole in me," he said, his voice a hoarse whisper that broke her heart. "One that my mom left behind."

Nora stroked his hair, not saying a word. She didn't want to pity him, something she hated when directed at her. She didn't offer meaningless platitudes or hollow promises. She just held him, touching him, letting him breathe. Hoping he knew she wouldn't judge him.

"I tried to fill it with the Air Force. I joined as soon as I turned eighteen."

"Did it help?"

"Yeah." He sighed. "For a while anyway. Then I tried to fill it with relationships."

She waited and waited. "But?" she prodded when he remained quiet.

"I never connected with anyone. No one came into my life that I felt the need to hold on to. That I couldn't live without."

This man was *not* a big sharer. A tiny part of her wanted to believe that he was only this way with her, telling her so much because maybe they had a connection. But she didn't dare allow herself to believe such a thing.

Not yet.

These were abnormal conditions. They'd been thrown together. She was his assignment. He was her bodyguard. Forced proximity in a safe house that was his home, with high stress mixed in. A life and death situation that made them both vulnerable.

Bo was the first man she felt like she could risk getting close to and yet, at the same time, forming an emotional bond with this man under these circumstances wasn't smart.

Was any of it real? If they were dating, like two normal people, would they have this closeness?

He was quiet for so long that she wondered if he was going to say more.

"Then I got out," Bo said, "and the guys at IPS and the Strattons and Logan, even Declan, they became my family."

Strattons? "Autumn has siblings?"

"Two sisters. Winter is with Chance and Summer is engaged to Logan. They're having an official engagement party next week."

All three sisters named after the seasons. For some reason, it made Nora smile. "Who's Declan?" No one else had mentioned him.

"Declan Hart is Winter's coworker. They're both DOJ Division of Criminal Investigation agents. He worked with Logan and Summer on a murder investigation of someone close to them. After that, those two fell in love and moved here. Her sisters followed. Somewhere along the way, Declan was included in our get-togethers. Now he's a part of our pseudofamily."

"Sounds nice. To find a family even if you can't be with the one you were born into." She didn't move, keeping her arm around him and stroking his hair. It felt good to hold him. To feel the weight of his body pressing down on her. Steady. Solid. So warm. His muscles relaxed even more as he nuzzled his face into the curve of her neck. "Does having them fill the hole?"

"In a way."

But not really.

"I'm still missing something in my life," he said.

Nora didn't know how to respond. She was missing so much in hers—stability, friends, family, love—that her life resembled Swiss cheese. "I can relate. The murders in Cold Harbor—hearing my friends murdered—when he almost got me into that van, being attacked in my college dorm... Every incident was a brutal blow, breaking something inside of me. Leaving pieces that I can't glue back together," she whispered, and Bo nuzzled closer, tightening an arm around her. "Sometimes I feel more like a ghost than a person. No connections. No bonds." No anchors. Constantly drifting. No roots. No place to call home. "Whenever I've left a place, I doubt people noticed I was gone or even missed me. Not that I blame them. I'm the one who always keeps myself at a distance, too terrified to get close to anyone. To care so deeply I wouldn't be able to leave if I had to."

"The way you were prepared to run at the office."

She nodded. "It's been really hard. Really lonely."

"I'm sorry I dumped all of that on you with everything you're going through."

"I'm not," she murmured into his ear. "Please, don't be."

"It sounds selfish."

"No, it doesn't. People don't share things with ghosts. It felt human. Personal." Exactly what she needed.

"The guys don't know any of that. It's not stuff I talk about."

Holding each other close, she smiled and kissed the top of his head, her hand caressing his cheek. The rough texture of his five o'clock shadow, more like eleven now, tickled her fingers and made her sigh. "Thank you for telling me. Trusting me." She'd poured her guts out to him since they first met and she was glad he opened up to her.

When he came to the hospital with follow-up questions after she'd been shot, she'd confided in him that she didn't have a ride home. No one in her life to turn to. On the drive to her house, he'd been so easy to talk to that she'd blabbered nonstop. He had escorted her to the front door and hesitated. There was a moment—a shared look, a charged tension building. The kind that told her a guy was interested. And she'd thought—*no*, she'd hoped—he'd ask her out on a date.

But then he didn't, and she told herself that it was for the best.

Rules kept her alive. Turning down dates and offers to grab coffee or see movies were done to prevent emotional ties. No sticky threads binding her to a place. Not when she might have to leave if she sensed danger.

She wanted this to be different. For all the long glances

with him—the little touches and kisses they'd shared that seemed to soothe and set off sparks for them both—to mean something.

But how could she trust her feelings as long as he was forced to have her there and she was a professional obligation?

His fingers slipped into her hair and played in her curls and his lips brushed her throat in a kiss. Gently. Tenderly.

Excitement rippled over her skin. Questions and doubts evaporated. There was something real between them. Even if it was only chemistry or attraction.

He eased her worries, listened and made her feel safe when no one else ever had. And she wanted to do the same for him. For however long their circumstances lasted.

"I'm so sorry he hurt you," he whispered, and the remorse in his voice gripped her heart. "What can I do? Anything to make it better?"

"Just hold me, Bo. Let me stay with you like this tonight." *Warm and safe in your arms.*

"I'm not too heavy on you?"

"No." Just the right amount of heavy. The right amount of strength. The right amount of sweet.

Being with him just felt right.

Leaning in, she pressed her lips to his brow, wishing she were kissing his mouth instead. An ache trickled through her entire body, pooling in her belly and coiling even lower. She wanted to get closer to him, feel his skin on hers, to touch him everywhere, to be touched in return.

A vague awareness of sexual frustration, something she'd never experienced and had only heard about, set in like an itch in the back of her mind. She yearned for the raw intimacy that could only be found in the arms of another.

Maybe one day.

Maybe with him.

Not because she was curious. Not because he was convenient. There was something about Bo that made her want to lose herself completely in his heat and his touch. She pressed her cheek to his head and ran her fingers over his spine.

He wrapped an arm around her waist and nuzzled against her. "I've got you, Nora," he said, and the words sounded like a vow.

Perhaps they had each other and that was how she'd get through this nightmare. With him.

Regardless, she was going to cling to his promise in her heart.

Chapter Ten

The smell of sugar cookies and sunshine curled around him. Then Bo woke with a start, his heart skipping a beat.

Nora was gone from the sofa, no longer beneath him. Her scent had also faded. His hand went to his hip. His weapon wasn't there either.

The shades were drawn. It was dark outside. The only light in the room was from the Christmas tree that was still on.

His mind raced. He tried to remember what had happened. He jackknifed up and a blanket slid down, falling to the floor.

"Nora!" his voice was hoarse and heavy.

"I'm here," she said behind him.

He whirled on the sofa to see her sitting at the table, sipping from a mug.

"Do you want coffee?" she asked. "I just brewed a pot."

Bo looked around the dimly lit space. There was a pillow on the sofa. She must've propped it under his head. The coffee table was clear. "Where's my gun?"

"On the side table. You shifted in the night and your weapon dug into my side, so I took it off you and set it there. Is that okay?"

That was not like him at all. He always secured his gun

before he fell asleep. Even more disturbing was that she had gotten up, removed his gun and placed a pillow under his head, all without him waking. "Yeah. It's okay."

They had been snuggled up together, cozy in front of the fire. She was soft and warm and smelled good. He'd been incredibly turned on, wanting to touch her and taste her, the memory of kissing her seared into his brain. But more than anything he needed to simply be close to her while not making another mistake.

She had wanted the same and he'd taken the comfort, a night of closeness and connection.

Goodness, he'd never opened up like that before, letting his guts spill out all over the place. Ugly. Messy. Showing pieces of himself that he wasn't proud to share. The things he'd told her... And after everything he'd said, she wanted to hold him.

To *sleep* with him.

Not have sex, or make love, but they had been far more intimate last night than he had ever been with any of his previous lovers, and they didn't even kiss on the sofa.

Bo didn't sleep with women. Sure, he dated, but he never invited anyone to stay the night. With his work schedule of early mornings, late evenings and short-notice deployments, that arrangement suited him. He was blunt and direct from the beginning, careful to never mislead anyone. A few women had pushed for more, but they had accepted what he was prepared to give until they were ready to move on. No broken hearts. No hurt feelings. Though his last girlfriend had cried when he told her he had no interest in continuing a long-distance relationship but that he wished her every happiness.

He had only been assigned to protect Nora for less than forty-eight hours and they'd slept together. More significantly, he'd wanted to and enjoyed it. Granted, they had been on the sofa, fully clothed, with her nestled beneath him and his head pillowed between her breasts. Still, they'd shared personal things, stuff he'd never confided to another soul.

To be honest, he hadn't given anyone else a chance.

Bo waited to be filled with shame for baring his soul to her, but he wasn't. He didn't feel regret and was not the least bit unsettled. He took it as a testament to how comfortable he already was with her. How much he trusted her.

Every time he'd been near Nora—this knockout, who was smart and mysterious—that magnetic thing between them pulled him to her. He didn't understand. It might as well have been a jigsaw puzzle that he had to figure out while blindfolded. A hundred different confusing pieces that could not possibly fit and in trying to, he risked getting his heart broken. But then last night, they talked—truly shared, touched each other deeply—and every single piece snapped together.

She had a vulnerability, a fragility about her that he recognized within himself. The loneliness. That black hole. It sucked him in, spoke to something deep inside him, drawing him to her. He realized now that it wasn't just her beauty or the fact that he was attracted to her. They both had similar wounds, and when he was around her, she soothed him, eased the gnawing ache.

Their current circumstances complicated everything. She was a client. An assignment. He could not live with himself if he failed her.

Nora was special. One of a kind.

Once this job was done and she was safe, he wanted to follow this connection and see where it could lead.

"What time is it?" he asked, stretching his arms.

She got up from the table and went to the kitchen cabinet. "Seven thirty."

"Goodness." He yawned. "I can't believe I slept so long." Or so well.

Grabbing the coffeepot, she filled a mug. "I guess you must've needed it."

Maybe he had. The night before, he hadn't slept much, if at all, worrying about the package that had been delivered and about how it had upset Nora. Bo'd been exhausted and had fallen asleep easily pressed against her.

"How about you?" he asked. "Were you able to get any rest with me on top of you like a chopped down log?"

Her lips curved as she handed him the mug. "I got solid sleep until a little after six. I tried to be quiet because I didn't want to wake you."

"Thanks." He gestured to the coffee and took a sip. Burned his tongue. "Hot."

"I should've warned you. Sorry."

He shrugged. "What is on the agenda for today?"

"A bunch of house showings, starting at nine." She picked up her phone and scrolled. "I logged into the system once I had my first cup of coffee to double-check everything on the schedule. Two more appointments were added last night. We have six right now, but that could change."

Bo frowned.

"What's wrong?" she asked.

"I don't like changes."

"Well, I have this picky family today and they're probably going to add new houses to the list or refuse to see ones I've selected for them. We need to be flexible with changes."

"Not that kind." Bo rubbed his jaw, his day-old stubble itched. He needed to shave.

She arched her brows. "Then what's the problem?"

"The two last-minute appointments." He blew on his coffee and sipped it. "Do you recognize the names? Have you shown them houses before?"

"No, they're both new."

New meant unvetted. "I don't like it." She got attacked, the assailant got away and now she had new clients who could really be anyone. Unexpected changes plus this coincidence were cause for concern. At minimum, extra precautions.

"Fairly common in real estate."

Maybe. "Even in mid-December? Doesn't business usually slow down by now?"

"Usually, yes, but like I said, I have this family who are relocating to the area and the teens are quite vocal about what they do and don't like. Also, I have two owners who are eager to sell. I'm grateful to have anyone willing to come out and see their houses. And one person is looking for an agent to show them two places."

"Do you have the addresses?"

"Yep. For the houses people have specifically requested to see." She came around the sofa and sat next to him. "Bearing in mind that the—"

"Fussy family of four is prone to making changes."

Grinning, Nora nodded. "Exactly." She held up her phone, showing him the real estate company app.

He could have taken it from her hand to look at it, but he leaned in to see the screen, his shoulder brushing hers.

She put her hand on his thigh.

Bo tensed, not wanting a resurgence in the excitement the lower part of his body had shown when she touched him last night. Lying on his side, he'd been able to hide his arousal, but he'd woken up still thinking of her, hungry for her instead of breakfast.

He sat beside her in the dim light of the Christmas tree. The room was warm and quiet and had him craving more of this intimacy. He scrolled through the addresses, inhaling her scent and letting it calm him. This morning, she was all natural. Gone was the smell of sugar cookies, but the scent of sunshine was pure Nora.

He glanced over at the app. "Which two names are new?" he asked, and she pointed them out.

The ten a.m. and five p.m. appointments, sandwiched in between the family.

She slid her palm along his thigh, and his brain scrambled like eggs in a hot pan.

Covering her hand with his, he stopped the sensual caress of his leg. "You're killing me, here."

"Oh." She let out a small chuckle. "I thought you'd like it. Should I stop?"

No, don't stop. "I do love it, Nora. A little too much. Makes it hard to focus on work because all I can think about is you and…"

She smiled, her gaze searching his face. "And?"

"How much I want to touch you. Hold you. Kiss you. But doing any of that will distract me from doing my job."

The smile on her face abruptly disappeared. "Wasn't last night nice? Don't you want to do that again?"

Drawing in a deep breath, Bo wrestled between complete honesty and what he thought he should say. "Yes." The truth won.

"Don't you want *more than* just that?"

Hell, yes. "I want you, but I need to do my job. To keep you safe."

"Do both. It doesn't have to be one or the other."

Sighing, he lowered his head. He'd give anything for both. To have her and protect her. This was his fear from the beginning—failing at one because he endeavored for the other. "If only it were that simple."

"It can be as simple as we choose to make it." She caressed his cheek and tilted his face back up to hers. "I have a proposal. While we're out there, it's business as usual, and we both focus on our jobs. But later, when we're back here, locked away in the safe house, we give ourselves permission to set the professional aside and get personal." She leaned in, and he thought she might kiss him, but she stopped a hair's breadth away, putting her forehead to his. "Spending time with you last night in that way helped me push away the ugliness and fear and forget," she whispered, her breath brushing his lips. "You gave me exactly what I didn't know I needed. Even if it was only for a few hours."

"You needed me crying on your shoulder?"

She stroked his cheek, her fingertips tickling his skin, and stared into his eyes. "Maybe. Focusing on you made me feel useful. Instead of helpless and afraid."

"You're strong and capable. You didn't need me to rescue you yesterday." She did that all by herself.

"But I did. Fighting. Surviving. That's not enough. It's not living. You rescued me from the darkness that haunts me every night." Her lips parted on a sigh, and he longed to kiss her. "Besides, you did say you would do anything to make me feel better."

Nora was a persuasive woman. She knew precisely how to push his buttons. Not that he needed much convincing.

"Okay." He swiped her curls off her face and behind her ear and ran his hand down her arm. "We'll give it a try," he said. Pulling back, she beamed at him, and it was like a sucker-punch to the solar plexus. He could barely breathe. She was so beautiful. The only mission he wanted was to make her smile like that every single day. "But right now, I have to be in work mode. I'm going to see what I can find out about the two new individuals before the appointments."

Straightening, she pulled her hands into her lap. "Understood. I'll stay out of your way." She rose from the sofa. "How about I make us breakfast while you do your bodyguard thing?"

"Sounds good. I could eat." He was starving, but he wanted more than food. Staring at her, he wasn't sure if he did a good job of hiding the hunger from his eyes.

"If you keep looking at me like that, it'll be hard for either of us to work."

Guess he got his answer. Averting his eyes, he nodded. "You're right."

"I'm going to shower," she said, her voice husky.

His thoughts tumbled straight to the gutter.

Get a grip, Lennox.

Refusing to watch her walk away, no matter how tempting her body was, he stared at the two new names on the list.

They couldn't afford any more surprises.

Chapter Eleven

To Nora's relief, her first appointment at nine turned out to be legitimate. A couple of empty nesters looking to downsize from their house and buy a new condo overlooking Bitterroot Lake while the developer offered a holiday discount.

After two other appointments that had already been in the books, they spent the rest of the day with the Grice family.

"What do you think?" Nora asked as they all finished touring the fifth house of the day and gathered in the living room.

Mr. Grice stroked his jaw as his wife shrugged. Not good signs.

Bo went over to the corner near the front door and flicked on the light. The sun was already setting and it was starting to get dark in the house. He gave Nora a furtive glance and tapped at his wrist, indicating the time, even though he wasn't wearing a watch.

Nora nodded, well aware this was taking far too long, as usual. She strolled closer to him to get another whiff of him. He smelled sexy. That aftershave he wore boosted his appeal to irresistible—masculine, earthy mixed with a hint of musk, but subtle. The scent was addictive, making it hard to stay focused on her difficult clients.

"Well, I think this isn't going to work," the sixteen-year-old daughter said, stomping into the empty living room, the sound of her boots echoing off the walls. "It's not fair if he gets a bigger bedroom than me."

The burly father crossed his arms. "Your brother is older," he said with a firm tone.

"By thirteen months! That doesn't make it fair. Besides, I'm the one who always makes honor roll. I have a 4.0 GPA."

"And your brother plays football." The mother studied the living room, and Nora hoped the woman was imagining her furniture filling out the space. "While getting good grades, even if it's not a 4.0."

The girl huffed. "Our rooms should be the same size."

In a perfect house they would be. Nora swallowed the words dancing on the tip of her tongue. She was beginning to wonder if this family was ever going to pull the trigger and buy something.

"There's only one extra bathroom and I don't want to share with her." The brother hiked his thumb back at his younger sister. Always wearing his varsity jacket, he had made it known multiple times he was going to hate living in a state that didn't have its own NFL team. "She's going to hog up all the counter space with her endless sea of products."

Bo rolled his eyes as a grumble rattled in his chest, and Nora was grateful that no one else was close enough to him to hear it. She hoped not anyway.

She shared his frustration. Someone in the family had an issue with every house—usually more than one person.

If Nora didn't find a way to wrap this up soon, they were going to be late for their next appointment. She plastered on a patient smile. "I really do think one of the new builds would suit your needs better. Aside from the primary bedroom, the others tend to be about the same size, and in these older homes you're going to get fewer bathrooms. I'd be happy to line up something for you to see tomorrow."

Sighing, the mother waltzed around, staring at the ceiling. "But look at this crown molding. It's gorgeous. We just won't find this level of detail in a newer house. I want our home to have character."

The real estate buzzword Nora dreaded—*character*. Clients looking for the character of an older home invariably also wanted the amenities of a newer one: updated appliances and plumbing, bigger bedrooms, extra bathrooms, fewer repairs.

Holding her fake smile in place, Nora nodded. "The molding is divine, but no house is going to have everything. I think we need to find the right compromise between charm and functionality," she said, keeping her tone light. No client wanted a lecture.

"Can you show us a house like this one?" the father asked. "But with an extra bathroom and one that needs fewer updates. Not finished, mind you, because I still want to put my stamp on it."

Of course, he did. Would a rubber stamp work? She could pick one up from the arts and crafts shop and Mr. Grice could stamp away until his heart was content.

"And I need a bigger bedroom," the Grice princess added.

"Certainly," Nora said, wishing she had a magic wand to make their impossible request a reality. "I'll see what I can find, but as I've told you, inventory is limited right now. Unless you're willing to wait indefinitely, I strongly suggest you reconsider looking at a new construction home. You could move in before the kids start school in January. No updates to worry about. All the bedrooms will be good in size. Your teens won't have to share a bathroom. Large windows with plenty of natural lighting. And, Mrs. Grice, you can always add little touches to the house to give it personality and Mr. Grice, I'm sure we can find a project for you so you can make it your own."

"Please, Mom," the daughter begged, pressing her palms together and making a pouty face.

"Makes the most sense." The son shoved his hands in his pockets. "We all get what we want that way. Let's at least look at it."

The woman's mouth twitched. "I don't know. I really have my heart set on a house with character. Not some cookie-cutter new build."

Bo put a palm on the small of Nora's back and patted, signaling her to hurry things along. Her cheeks heated, and for a second, she found it hard to think about anything but the feel of his hand on her, wishing it would slide a little lower and that they had on fewer clothes while he touched her.

Glancing over her shoulder at him, she bit back a smile and mouthed, *Okay.* Then she turned back to the family. "I'll send you a link so you can take a look at the photos of a couple of additional homes that I have in mind. Builders are offering good deals at this time of year. You could shave off thousands from the list price of a new build." She moved toward the door. Thankfully they followed. "If you want to see them, just give me a call or you can go through the office to set up an appointment."

They thanked her, mumbled good-byes and left as they continued to debate the pros and cons of the houses they'd seen.

"Why do folks bring their kids along?" Bo asked. "It only seems to make the process harder."

Grabbing her coat from the hook, she shrugged. "At least the teenagers think new construction makes sense." Made them the more reasonable ones to her. Too bad they weren't the ones with the money. "I think it's nice how the parents take their kids' opinions into consideration." While it was unusual for her to manage the entire family, the Grice couple had pulled their teens from school early before the Christmas break since they would be attending a new high school in Montana at the start of the year. "My mom and Pa never would have, but I think it's kind of sweet." Albeit a tad frustrating.

Bo scowled. "And I think it's a big headache listening to four opinionated voices when only two are going to pay the mortgage."

Chuckling, she unzipped her purse, moved some things around and frowned.

"What's wrong?" he asked, concern in his voice.

"I can't find my phone. I was going to text the next appointment and let Dr. Hiller know we're running behind a few minutes."

Bo lifted his hand. He was holding her phone. "You left it on the counter in the kitchen."

"Oh, I didn't realize." She took it from him and headed out the door.

He was right behind her. "You set it down when you started showing them the appliances. From an operational security perspective, it's best to leave it in your purse and carry your handbag with you."

Bo even made the phrase *operational security* sound sexy.

"I do keep my purse close." With her loaded gun tucked inside. "But if my cell phone is stuck in my bag, sometimes it's hard to hear a text when I'm busy trying to sell or during an open house when a home is filled with people."

She locked up the place and they got into the truck.

Bo pulled off for her next showing. She sent a text to her

potential new client, hating to make a bad first impression by being late. The Grice family consistently ran over their allotted time with their hemming and hawing. Nora just didn't have the heart to hurry them along when they could be purchasing their forever house.

"You have far more patience than I do," he said.

"That's not true." The first time he questioned her at the hospital after the mass shooting, she'd stonewalled him. Too terrified any cooperation would lead to her exposure. Turned out, her concern was misplaced and should've been solely directed at the press. "You've always been nothing but patient and kind with me." Being shot had been horrific and she had appreciated his compassion at a difficult time.

"Well, you're special." Glancing at her, he smiled, and her heart rolled over in her chest.

He pulled in front of the site of her next appointment. A ranch-style home that had a long, low profile with a low-pitched roof and wide eaves. The place featured stone and wood and had large windows to take advantage of the mountain views. The owners were only selling because of a recent divorce and hoped to start the new year with a fresh start.

"Looks like we beat Dr. Hiller," Bo said.

No other cars were parked at the house. "That's a relief. I'm glad I didn't have to make him wait." She climbed out of the truck. Her dress had hitched up a bit on the ride over, and she tugged it back down over her knees. "What did you find out about my potential new client?"

Bo came around to her side and took her arm, helping her walk over a patch of ice. "He's a dentist over in Cutthroat Creek. Fifty-nine years old. Balding. Blue eyes. Wears glasses. If someone other than a man meeting that description shows up to see this listing, I want you to make an excuse to go to the truck, get inside, take out your gun and drive straight to the police station." He handed her his keys. "Got it?"

"Yeah, sure, but Dr. Allan Hiller is a real person."

"Doesn't matter. Easy enough to look someone up on the internet and use their name to book an appointment. Especially since the guy who's after you knows you hired IPS."

Swallowing hard, she put his fob in her pocket as they headed up the driveway. "The place should be good to go, but I should do a quick walk through and I need to open all the curtains. It's a hassle to close them after every showing only to open them again, but the owners are worried about someone breaking in and stealing the copper pipes if thieves realize no one is living in the house."

"The owners already moved out?"

"Yeah. They're going through a divorce and with the holidays, they thought it would be easier this way. It's sad. They're such a nice couple."

"Not every relationship is forever."

She entered the code for the lockbox and grabbed the key. "What's your longest?"

"A year, but it never got serious."

How could you be with someone for a year without it getting serious? But she decided against asking the question. At least right now.

He put a hand on her back. "How about you?"

"I don't date. No attachments, remember?" Her hand trembled as she tried to get the key in the lock.

"Not ever? Not even in high school before everything happened?"

Before three of her friends were slaughtered while she was forced to listen to their screams.

"Uh, no. I was a late bloomer." *Dang it*. She couldn't get the key in. "No boyfriends."

"At all?" The surprise in his voice grated on her nerves.

"Nope." The keys slipped from her hand and clattered to the ground.

Bo bent down, picking up the keys for her. "I didn't realize you were so cold," he said.

That wasn't the reason she was shaking. Her throat tightened and a different kind of heat crept up her chest. She was ashamed that what rattled her wasn't the memory of her friends dying. The awkwardness stemmed from Bo finding out that she'd never had a real boyfriend. From him eventually connecting the dots to the fact she had never been intimate with a man.

He slipped one of the keys into the first lock, made quick work of the dead bolt and then handed her the keys.

"Thanks." She pushed the door open and switched on the light.

Her breath hitched and then she screamed, dropping the keys on the hardwood floor.

Chapter Twelve

"Oh, God!" Nora rushed into the living room before Bo could grab hold of her. "No, no, no. Amanda," she sobbed.

A redhead lay spread-eagle on the floor, shirt ripped open and covered in blood.

"Stop, Nora!" He managed to snatch her arm and haul her back before she stepped in the blood that had pooled and congealed on the floor around the body. Spinning her around, he brought her in against his chest and held her, keeping her face turned away.

"Is she dead?" she said, her voice so low it was barely audible.

There was no doubt in his mind that the woman was dead and had been for several hours. "I need you to go outside and call 911."

"Amanda. Is she dead?" Nora asked again.

"Yes," he said, softening his tone. He stroked her hair, trying to be as gentle as possible. "She's dead."

Nora cried harder, and he tightened his arms around her.

On the bright white wall, written in blood, were two words: *ANOTHER MINNOW*.

Bo's gaze dropped back to the body. "How do you know her?"

"She..." Her voice broke on a sob. "I work with her. Amanda. She's a real estate agent."

Two women dead in two days—both people Nora knew well. A neighbor and now a coworker.

Bo kissed the top of her head. "Listen to me," he said firmly. "Step away over there and call the police. Tell them to notify Detective Powell."

She didn't move.

"Nora." He sharpened his voice. "I need you to do it now."

She glanced up, her watery, shocked gaze meeting his. Giving him a solemn nod, she backed away toward the door and stayed where he could see her.

Bo pulled latex gloves from his pocket. When he was working on a job, he always carried a pair, along with his weapon and some zip ties. No telling if they might come in handy. He dragged on the gloves. Only as a precaution since he had no intention of touching anything. He crouched for a better look at the dead body without getting too close.

She'd been stabbed several times. From what he could see, at least ten wounds. The medical examiner might find more under the blood. There was so much of it on the walls, the floor and covering the woman's torso. Her skin was gray.

Bruises covered her throat. Although her limbs were spread apart, her ankles and wrists had duct tape around them. Like the killer had cut her loose once she was dead and repositioned the body. A strip of black tape also covered her mouth. He didn't want the neighbors to hear her scream.

Bo turned his attention to Nora, who was staring down at the horrific scene, her eyes glazed, her expression shaken. The phone was in her hand, hanging at her side. She was in no condition to call the police.

A woman came up the walkway and gasped. "Oh, dear heaven."

Holding up a palm, Bo went to the doorway to keep the woman from running into the house. "Please, step back, ma'am. You have to stay outside." Gaping at him, the gray-haired woman nodded as he dialed 911.

The emergency services operator answered.

"This is Bo Lennox with Ironside Protection Services. I need to report a homicide." He passed along the address and responded to all the operator's questions. "I have reason to believe this is related to an ongoing investigation and request that Detective Logan Powell be notified as soon as possible."

The older woman had caught the attention of a neighbor, who flagged down another person. The houses were clustered close together and this was prime time for folks to get home from work. In a matter of minutes, a crowd was gathering outside.

Bo went to Nora, tugging off his gloves before putting an arm around her. Guiding her out of the house, he stood guard against inquisitive onlookers who had begun to converge. He pulled the door nearly shut, only leaving a crack. Holding Nora, he shielded her face, putting her cheek to his chest.

Then he fired off a quick text to the IPS group chat with the address and added four words.

Second victim. Here now.

Whoever was available would come, but he needed to make sure one person hightailed over there. He dialed Logan's cell. "Has dispatch notified you yet?" he asked once his friend picked up.

"Notified me about what?"

Clenching his jaw, Bo had his answer and didn't like it. "I'm going to text you an address. I need you here right now."

"I'm already in my truck. Just tell me the address," Logan

said, and Bo gave it to him. "What's up? Has something happened?"

"There's a body," he said low, hyperaware of the people standing within earshot, hoping to get any morsel of information they could use for gossip. "Nora and I found her." Precisely the way the Yuletide Killer had planned.

Logan sucked in a harsh breath and swore. "I'm on my way. Not far from you."

Turning to the growing crowd outside the house, Bo waved people back. "Please stand on the sidewalk. The police will be here soon. The easier we make it for them to get inside, the better."

Slowly, they listened to him, to his surprise.

"Bo, do you know who the victim is?" Logan asked on the other end of the phone.

"One of Nora's coworkers. A real estate agent. Amanda. I don't know her last name."

"Collins," Nora said, her voice shaky, racked with sobs.

"Amanda Collins. I already called it in to 911 and requested that they inform you. The police should be here any minute."

"I'll notify dispatch that I'm en route, two minutes away, but in case a patrol officer beats me there, I don't want anyone to disturb the crime scene until I arrive. How is Nora holding up? First her neighbor, then an attack on her and now this?"

"About what you'd expect," he said. She was trembling against him, softly weeping, teeth chattering. "She's in shock."

"See you soon." Logan disconnected.

Bo slipped his phone into his pocket and focused on Nora, drawing her closer. All he could do was hold her while she completely broke down.

"How many more?" Her hands grasped at his coat. She looked up at him, her cheeks wet, tears streaming down her face. "How many more lives is he going to take?"

At a loss for a response, Bo shook his head. He had no idea. Nora had gone to great lengths not to get close to anyone and yet, somehow, this monster had managed to hone in on the few individuals in Nora's orbit.

More will die, Nora's attacker had said. *More minnows will bleed*.

"Were you close with Amanda? I realize you weren't hanging out at her house and having spa days together, but I mean relatively speaking."

"Not really. She was always chatty with me in the office and talked about everything. Listings. Church. Her love life or lack thereof. A couple of weeks ago, we had an office holiday party, which was just dinner at a restaurant. Joe, the lead agent, started making it mandatory because I would never go."

"Which restaurant?"

"The Wolverine Lodge. It was the office manager, Tad, and the three of us agents. After dinner, she asked me to stay a little longer. Have a drink with her. She really pushed me and I caved."

Nora wept harder, covering her mouth with her hand as if to mute the sounds coming from her. He tucked her head under his chin and held her.

They must've misjudged the situation from the beginning and got it all wrong. This perverse man must have been watching Nora for weeks. Waiting. Preparing. Anticipating that she would refuse to play his game. Planning who he would kill to punish her. To make her suffer.

All this time the danger hadn't only been to Nora. Now

her neighbor and coworker were both dead. Collateral damage. And the killer's identity was still a mystery to them.

This monster had brutally murdered two women and wanted to do the same to Nora. They had to find him.

Bo stroked her hair and kissed her forehead.

Nora stared up at him, her eyes turning hard despite the tears still flowing. "We have to stop him," she whispered. "Before he kills anyone else."

"I know." They were playing defense with a bloodthirsty devil when they needed to be on the offense. "Maybe the only way to do that is to take the fight to him."

She blinked at him. "But how?"

"I think we have to go back to where it all started."

"Home?" she asked, pulling back with a shudder. "Go back to Cold Harbor?"

He nodded. "Yes."

A silver Dodge Ram with red and blue flashing lights on the dash screeched to a halt and a patrol cruiser stopped behind him. Logan got out, followed by two officers. They proceeded to get the crowd under better control. The uniformed cops instructed the curious neighbors, some who were on the phone and most likely spreading word, to back away from the property and into the street or to return to their homes.

Bo hoped he could get Nora out of there before any reporters showed up. He didn't want her to have to face the media or intrusive questions or to have her face splashed all over the news again. She'd already been through enough.

She put her forehead on his chest. "I need this nightmare to end."

"I know," he said gently, stroking her hair. "We're going to make that happen. Find him. Put an end to this." One way or another.

"He stabbed her. So many times." A sob stuck in her throat. "Why? Just to hurt her?" She was crying again, and he wanted to ease her hurt. "To make her suffer?"

"I wish I knew." He wondered if the crime scene at Mrs. Moore's had been similar.

"And her throat, Bo." She took a shaky breath as she wept. "Did he strangle her, too?"

He held her and rubbed her back, to comfort and warm her. "I believe so. Yes."

As Logan made his way to them, Bo spotted Autumn parking her vehicle.

"I'm going to need to ask you some questions before you leave," Logan said to him.

"I figured." Bo nodded. "Give me a minute."

Logan pulled on gloves and glanced over his shoulder at the crowd. "Hey, let Dr. Stratton through," he said to the officers while gesturing to Autumn. "She's with IPS." Then he disappeared inside the house.

Taking one of Nora's hands, he held it. "I'm sure someone has notified the news station by now. They could be here at any minute, and I don't want you around when the reporters descend."

Autumn hurried over and gave Nora's arm a sympathetic pat. "I got here as fast as I could. Eli is on the way, too. Tak is busy with a client."

"Can you take her to your car?" Bo asked. "Lock the doors. Get her warm. I think she's still in shock. When E gets here, take her to my place." Since Autumn didn't have tactical training, he wanted her to wait for backup. His house was secure, but anything could happen on the ride over with this savage murderer on the loose. "I don't want her here and I'm not sure how long it'll take with Logan." Bo needed to tell Logan everything he knew and get questions of his own answered before he could be with Nora.

"Yeah, sure," Autumn said.

Nora didn't protest. She looked like she was going to be sick.

Autumn and Eli would take good care of her until he got to the house. He was thankful Nora would have the emotional support of a skilled psychologist to confide in if she needed to talk. The past two days had been riddled with fear and trauma for her.

He glanced at his teammate. With Autumn's puffy coat, Bo couldn't tell if she had her weapon on her. "Are you carrying?"

"We have a murderer stalking a client." She glared at him. "Of course."

It should've gone without saying, but he had to be certain. "Sorry."

"I've looked at the case," she said, "and done a little digging. I have some thoughts. When there's time, we should discuss it."

"Yeah. I want to hear what you've found." Autumn had been instrumental in helping them find the sniper from the mass shooting. Though she moved here to slow down after burning out in Los Angeles, cases kept finding her and she couldn't resist diving into them. It was a good thing, too, because her talent would be wasted if she was sitting on the sidelines. "Let me get through this first."

An ambulance turned down the street, lights flashing, siren off. It was protocol for them to be here.

The crowd had swelled to at least a dozen. More than one person held their phone up—taking video footage or pictures or waiting for the dead body to be removed.

"I'll walk you to the car. Nora, keep your head down.

Autumn and I will do our best to block the crowd's view of your face as we go."

He glanced at Autumn, and she nodded that she was ready.

He kept his arm around Nora and she angled her cheek toward his chest and shielded the rest of her face using her hand. With Autumn blocking the view of her from the other side, he hoped it was enough to prevent her name and face from making the news.

As they headed across the snow-covered lawn, Eli arrived, pulling in beside Autumn's vehicle. *Perfect timing.*

"Let's get her into Eli's truck," Autumn suggested and opened the passenger's side door.

Bo took his key fob from Nora's coat pocket and helped her climb inside the cab of the truck. He stepped up on the running board. "Hey, E. Take her to my place. Autumn is going to follow. I've got to talk to Logan."

"Yeah, no problem."

From the corner of his eye, Bo noticed Sierra Shively from Forensics getting out of her vehicle and marching up to the house.

He cupped Nora's cheek. "I'm going to check in with you," he whispered. No need to make sure she was safe because he was confident that E and Autumn wouldn't let anything happen to her, but he didn't want her to feel like he'd simply left her after yesterday's incident at the church.

"Will you be gone long?" she asked.

"Only as long as necessary. Okay?"

Her throat worked as she swallowed and nodded.

He swiped his fingers over her cheeks to dry them from her tears and kissed her forehead. It wasn't until afterward that he realized touching her had become a reflex somewhere along the way. He wondered what Eli would think of how close he'd gotten to Nora. What his friend would have to say about it. He also realized that he didn't care. She needed him and he intended to be there for her in every way possible. Bo would simply have to deal with a lecture later.

"Thanks," he said to Eli, who was looking at him with narrowed eyes, his gaze bouncing between him and Nora.

E gave a slow nod.

Bo climbed down and shut the door.

Autumn was already in her SUV, prepared to leave.

He lifted his hand in a quick wave and watched their vehicles take off, navigating the congested street.

The two uniformed officers at the scene knew him and let him pass without a problem. IPS had developed a good reputation. They worked hard to cultivate a positive relationship with the authorities and it helped that Detective Powell was already there.

Putting on his gloves, he stalked back to the house and went inside.

Shively was taking photos of the dead body, her mouth set in a grim line while she worked.

"Did Nora leave?" Logan asked when Bo joined him in the living room.

"Yeah." Bo's temple throbbed. He should take something to fight back the headache beginning to pound in his skull, but he wanted to get through this. "Autumn and Eli are taking her to my house. They'll stay with her until I can get there."

"I asked Winter for a favor—to run the DNA evidence we got off Nora yesterday through the DCI lab. Faster than ours. We should know something by tomorrow." Logan stared down at Amanda Collins with a stony expression and pointed to the upper part of her body. "She was strangled and stabbed. Same as Mrs. Moore."

"Same level of..." He searched for the right word. "Gore?"

"The scene was worse with her elderly neighbor. The woman's ring finger was severed. I didn't want to mention the gruesome detail in front of Nora." Logan shook his head, the hardened look on his face remaining unchanged except for his jaw tightening. "Not that what this scumbag did to Amanda is any less heinous."

Something about the way he said her name struck Bo. "Did you know her well?"

Logan gave a brief, curt nod, still studying the body with angry focus. "I knew her. But not very well. We weren't friends."

"Any idea how long she's been dead?" Bo asked.

"The ME will give us a time of death."

"Come on, Logan. I can tell it's been hours. Give me a rough estimate of how long."

The detective sighed on a shrug. "Around twenty-four hours would be my *rough* guess."

"Definitely sometime last night," Shively agreed. She lowered the camera and turned to them. "I bet no one has heard from her or seen her today. That's my two cents for what it's worth."

Bo nodded. "It all counts."

"There you go. Two unofficial opinions," Logan said. "You're welcome to come with me to the morgue and get a better estimate firsthand from the ME until the autopsy is done or I can let you know."

"Thanks. I'll tag along." The sooner they had more information, the better. He would give Nora a call in a few minutes to check in. Make sure she got to the house all right and update her on his plan to go to the morgue.

"No telling how long he had her before he killed her."

Logan indicated a stack of clothes neatly folded off to the side of the body. There were jagged cuts throughout the material like it had been slashed. "He cut off her coat and blazer."

"Did he do the same with Mrs. Moore?" Bo asked.

"Yeah," Logan said. "Folded them, too. This guy was just as thorough at the Moore place. He left the kitchen spotless. A boning knife cleaned and put in the dish drainer. No prints. He wiped the entire kitchen with bleach. The same type of knife is in the kitchen here. The only utensil in the house."

"Bleach, too?"

"The smell of it is potent in there, but I haven't seen any bleach or spray bottles on my preliminary check. I doubt I'll find any when I go back through."

"You're thinking he brought it with him?" Bo asked.

Another nod from Logan. "This was planned." He looked up at Bo. "Walk me through what happened with you and Nora."

"This morning, Nora checked her schedule, with an app the office uses. She had two new clients slated to view houses. One at ten and this one at five. I had a bad feeling about the last-minute additions after the attack on her at the church. Did my due diligence—looked up the names to see what I could find."

Logan took out his notebook and a pen. "Who was scheduled to meet her here?"

"A dentist from Cutthroat Creek. Dr. Allan Hiller. His office is closed today and I didn't have time to get his personal number to verify him because she had appointments starting first thing this morning." Then he remembered something. "Nora texted the number listed to say that we were running late. No response."

"Do you have the number?"

"Yeah." Bo took out his phone and gave it to him.

"The scumbag probably looked for an easily verifiable identity online. Someone local. Picked the dentist. Left a number to a burner phone for the appointment. But I'll check it out," Logan said. "Go on."

"As I was saying, we were running late. Maybe fifteen minutes. When we arrived, I noticed that there were no other cars parked outside," Bo said, thinking. "Which makes me wonder where Amanda's vehicle is. Do you think he nabbed her somewhere else and transported her here?"

"It's possible. I'll check with the real estate company to see if she had any late-day clients or missed any appointments. When Summer and I were looking to buy a house, we worked with Amanda. Very friendly. Far too trusting. She offered to drive us around in her car. I couldn't have her chauffeuring me around, so I drove the three of us. She might've gotten into the killer's car willingly, believing she was with a legitimate client. It would explain why there was no forced entry into the house."

"And the perp put the key back in the lockbox to make it appear as if everything was fine."

"So, you got here, and Nora got the key out of the box?"

Pinching the bridge of his nose, Bo nodded. The throbbing in his head was spreading. He needed to stop at the drugstore on his way home and pick up something for a tension headache. "Yeah, but her hands were shaking. She dropped the keys and I was the one who unlocked and opened the door."

"Any idea why she was shaking? Was she nervous about something? Did anything seem off before you got inside the house?"

Bo shrugged. "I think she was just cold." He thought back on it. "We were talking about, um, well, personal stuff." Her not having a boyfriend. Ever. Did that mean she'd never been intimate with anyone? "Nothing seemed odd or out of place outside. We went into the house. She turned on the lights and that's when we saw the body. The client was a no-show of course." A fake. "The whole thing was a setup. This grisly scene that he left for Nora."

"Was she friends with Amanda?"

"No. They were friendly, but they didn't socialize regularly. There was a company party. A couple of weeks ago at the Wolverine Lodge. It was the first time they hung out. Stayed after dinner at a restaurant and had drinks. Just the two of them. When she told me that, I realized he must've been watching her for weeks. We'll get the surveillance tapes from the restaurant. See if we spot anyone following Nora—watching her. It's the only way he could've figured out who she knows…who she might care about."

"Which deaths would hurt or rattle her the most," Logan said.

"I don't think he wants to simply kill Nora. Torturing her first is a part of this for him." Every detail of this twisted soul's plan was meticulously crafted. He wanted to ensure each moment of agony she experienced would be etched into her memory forever.

Was it simply for sick satisfaction?

Was it insurance that he would hurt her in the event she got away again?

Or was it to wear her down, to finally break her, so that she would give up on running altogether?

Bo looked back at Amanda's body. Bruised. Bloodied. Butchered. This could've been Nora.

It might still be Nora's fate if they didn't do something. Whatever the cruel devil's goal, Bo was determined to make sure he didn't succeed.

Chapter Thirteen

Nora answered the call on the first ring. "Hello."

"Are you all right?" Bo asked.

The sound of his voice on the other end of the phone calmed her nerves, the muscles in her tight shoulders loosening. She knew the update wouldn't be good since the last time they spoke—which was hours ago—he was on his way to the morgue, but talking to him eased her worries a bit.

"Yes. I'm fine. Still with Autumn and Eli. They're looking out for me. By the way, you're on speaker," Nora said, with her cell phone on the table so that Autumn and Eli, who were both in the kitchen with her, could hear. "What did you learn at the morgue?"

Bo didn't immediately answer, like he was deciding how much to tell her.

"You don't need to filter anything for my sake," Nora said. "I can handle it."

"The cause of death was asphyxiation. He stabbed Amanda to torture her. Then he strangled her. The rest of the stab wounds were done postmortem. Twelve cuts in all. It was the same with Mrs. Moore. I went back over the Cold Harbor police report. The girls weren't strangled, but they were each stabbed twelve times."

A shudder ran through Nora as the memory of her friends' screams echoed in her mind.

"I wonder if the number twelve is related to the twelve days of Christmas," Autumn said, "or has some other significance." The woman's gaze fell to her.

Nora shrugged. "I have no idea. At the time, the detectives thought it was an aspect of a ritual kill. I don't think they examined the specific number beyond that."

"I don't want you to focus on that right now," Bo said. "Rehashing everything. Tonight has been hard enough on you already."

"If only I had known that he might go after Amanda." Nora wiped at her eyes. "Maybe I could've warned her. We could've protected her somehow."

"Nora, you might've chosen not to have any friends to protect yourself," Bo said, "but you're friendly with lots of people. We can't protect half the town."

Her shoulders sagged under the weight of that realization. Autumn put a hand on her arm.

"ETA, man," Eli said.

"I should be there in thirty minutes. I need to stop at the drugstore on my way. Nora, I'll get there as soon as I can."

"I'll be waiting."

Bo ended the call.

Autumn slid the broth that Nora had been nursing closer.

Picking up the mug, Nora held the cup of warm liquid between both her hands and took another sip. Even though she'd told Autumn that she didn't want anything to eat or drink, Nora was glad to have listened to the doctor. Even if Autumn wasn't a medical doctor.

The broth settled Nora's stomach and warmed her up, getting rid of the tremors.

Autumn poured a cup of freshly brewed coffee for herself and sat at the kitchen table beside her with a sympathetic expression.

A delicious aroma permeated the kitchen. Eli was busy baking. Shortbread cookies. It took him twenty minutes to throw the simple ingredients together and pack the dough into a pan. With his arms crossed over his chest, he stood near the oven, waiting to take them out.

The smell of yummy goodness was almost strong enough to lighten her mood and steer her mind from something other than death, but then the image of Amanda's body flashed in her head again. She couldn't help but wonder if that was how the police had found Mrs. Moore. Brutalized and bloody.

All because Nora refused to obey a monster's orders.

"You can't blame yourself for these deaths," Autumn said, as if reading her mind. Once again trying to make Nora feel better by absolving her of any culpability. "The killer has engineered this sadistic game. All in an effort to manipulate you into doing what he wants. Shouldering any guilt, no matter how small, only empowers him over you. Don't do it."

Nora sipped the broth. "Easier said than done, Doc."

"None of what you've been through has been easy," Autumn said. "Coming out on the other side won't be either, but you've already suffered losses no person should have to endure. Your innocence. Your adolescence. Family and friends. Your freedom to grow and explore without fear. And despite it all, you're still a fighter. You can do this."

"I keep asking myself—how many more people have to die in order for me to live?" Nora set the mug down. "If he just takes me, then no one else will get hurt and this will end."

A timer Eli had set started beeping. He shut it off. "This

won't end until we catch this guy and make him pay in a court of law for everything he's done," he said, slipping on oven mitts. "Or we kill him. Either way works for me." The gritty tone as the big, muscular guy took cookies out of the oven formed an incongruous image. "Anything else is unacceptable." He placed the pan on top of the stove.

Autumn put a hand on her shoulder. "Eli is right. All of those victims—your friends, Mrs. Moore, Amanda Collins and you—deserve justice."

"I know this isn't my fault," Nora muttered, more to herself than to the others in the room.

"This is most certainly not your fault," Autumn said, making Nora blink up at her.

"I just..." Nora dropped her head into her hands, hating that she felt this way. "I just don't want any more deaths on my conscience."

Eli sliced the cookies with a knife. "Let IPS and the cops carry that burden. We have to do our jobs, which includes protecting you." He used a spatula to scoop some from the pan and put them on a plate. "Every day that killer is on the loose—every life he takes—it's on us. Not you."

"You've survived this killer's best efforts," Autumn said, "but he's taken so much from you already. Don't let him take anything else. Especially not your peace of mind during quiet moments when you can catch your breath. I want you to practice the three *R*s. Recharge. Recognize. Remember. You have to recharge your body and spirit. No one can run on fumes. Recognize the good things that happen and hold on to them. It's human nature to let the darkness overshadow the light in difficult times. I want you to battle against that inclination. Most importantly, you have to *remember* what you're fighting for. What do you want your life to look like when this is over?"

Nora stiffened. No one had ever asked her that before. She'd spent so long living like a ghost that she didn't have a clue what having a *real* life would look like. How it would feel. To be free instead of a prisoner to a madman's obsession.

She glanced up and they were both staring at her.

"Have a cookie," Eli ordered, popping the bubble of tension. He set the plate down on the table in front of her. "That's my mom's recipe. The secret is a tablespoon of milk. Makes them super soft unlike traditional shortbread. One of those will melt in your mouth. Guaranteed to banish the blues. Try one."

Her throat closed from the kindness they were showing her. If this was how they rallied around a pro bono client, someone they barely knew, she could only imagine what they would do for a friend or family. Bo was lucky to have them in his life to look out for him.

Nora glanced down at the cookies, tempted to take a nibble, but she wasn't ready to feel better. Not quite yet. She still couldn't believe Amanda was gone. Sweet, funny Amanda who had done nothing wrong. Who would never again get to sip broth and eat homemade cookies because she was dead.

Murdered.

"Thank you for going to the trouble to make the cookies." Nora was grateful for the distraction that kept her from overthinking or worse—crying. "I'll eat them. I promise. In a little bit. Okay?"

"Sure, no rush." With a compassionate look on his face, Eli nodded. "But they are sublime when warm." He picked one up and munched on it, making a face like he was in heaven.

Autumn followed suit. "Oh, my goodness, Eli. These

are fantastic." The enthusiasm on her face and in her voice was genuine.

"See?" Eli said to Nora. "I told you."

She offered them a grin. A fake one. She was in no way happy, but she wanted to show her appreciation for their efforts. To repay them somehow, even if it was only a forced smile.

The alert sounded, signaling someone was coming down the road.

Eli headed for the office. A moment later he called out from down the hall, "It's just Bo."

"Are you okay?" Autumn asked. "Feeling any better?"

Nora wasn't okay, but she would be. "You and Eli helped a lot." Autumn's perspective as a psychologist and Eli's baking. "The sooner we catch him, the sooner I can move on from this." For far too long, she had been this killer's prey.

She was sick of running and ached to take the fight to his doorstep.

The truck door slammed shut.

Her heartbeat picked up, something inside her already lightening in anticipation of seeing Bo.

As the dead bolt unlocked, there was a soft mechanical whir, and then the front door swung open.

Bo stepped inside and removed his coat. Nora's heart stuttered and she was out of her seat and wrapping her arms around him before he could take off his boots.

Giving her a hug, he tucked her head under his chin, and she immediately felt better with him there. She took in his scent—that enticing male smell along with his aftershave—and relaxed against him.

He eased back, propped a knuckle under her chin and tipped her face up to his. "Hey."

"Hey."

His brow furrowed. "You told me they were taking good care of you," he said, the question clear though unspoken.

"They have been. They're both amazing. Eli even baked cookies," she said, and his gaze flicked up to someone behind her, his expression turning unreadable. "I'm just glad you're back."

Autumn and Eli moved to the door and put on their shoes.

"Your phone calls made a difference," Autumn said. "Every time you checked in, she relaxed a little more."

Was she that obvious? Nora stepped away from Bo.

"It's late. Tomorrow, I can tell you what I've learned." Autumn slipped into her coat. "And we can go over my theories."

Bo nodded. "First thing in the morning. We can meet at IPS. The whole team. We can have Chance sit in on the meeting by phone. There's something I wanted to discuss, too."

"I need to talk to you," Eli said to Bo. "Privately." His entire demeanor changed from considerate baker to ticked-off guy with a chip on his shoulder.

Bo sighed. "It can wait until tomorrow."

"No, it can't." Eli folded his arms. "You don't even know what it's about."

"I've got a good idea and I'm not in the mood to hear it. Not tonight."

Autumn eyed them. "Is this a personal or professional matter?" the doctor asked.

Both men responded at the same time.

"Personal," Bo said.

"Professional." Eli narrowed his eyes at Bo.

Autumn rubbed her forehead, clearly fatigued. "It's almost midnight, Eli." Taking a breath, she rested a hand on Eli's shoulder. "We should both go. This discussion, whatever it's about, can wait until tomorrow. It's been a long day. Nora needs to rest. We all do."

Eli's jaw clenched and he hesitated a minute, but the man relented with a nod. "Fine. But we talk before the meeting."

"I'm fine with that," Bo said.

The tension between them was still thick.

Nora turned to Eli. "Thanks again for the cookies."

"You made me a promise. I hope you'll keep it."

She smiled. "I will."

A muscle twitched in Bo's cheek as his gaze slid from her to Eli.

Autumn gave Nora a one-armed hug. "Please get some sleep. Good night." The doctor left.

Eli snatched his coat from the hook. "Tomorrow," he reiterated, then stalked out into the cold.

Bo locked the door and slipped off his boots. Facing Nora, he took her hand and put her palm on his cheek. The faint scrape of his stubble anchored her. This was real. He was warm and solid and she could count on him to stick with her through this nightmare.

But what about when it was over?

What was she fighting for?

"What promise did you make Eli?" he asked, his tone gentle.

"Nothing special. Just that I would eat the cookies he made."

A grunt came from him. "That's his thing. Baking. It's how he takes care of people, processes things, relaxes, makes decisions. By baking treats. Not cooking, mind you," he said, and she smiled. "The guy subsists on pizza and spaghetti. Though, he does make a mean meatball." His voice still held a note of irritation.

She didn't know what was going on between him and his

friend, but she didn't want to talk about Eli. "What's your thing? Listening to music?"

"I guess." Shrugging, he went into the kitchen and washed his hands. "Never really thought about it. But listening to music is not as useful as baking."

"Depends on what you're doing while you're listening, I suppose."

"Do you want some milk to go with the cookies?" he asked, and she nodded. "Warm or cold?"

"Warm. I'll do it." She went to the cabinet that had the pots and pulled one out. "You want yours warm, right?"

"I do."

She grabbed milk from the fridge and poured enough for two in the pot and turned on the stove. "Play something for us."

After he put on sultry, smooth music, he built a fire. They met on the sofa. Nora handed him a mug and set the plate between them on the coffee table.

When she finally tried a cookie, her palate was completely unprepared for the divine mixture. A moan slipped from her. "This is incredible."

"Yeah. He's a great baker."

They enjoyed the cookies, listening to the music and drinking their milk.

She glanced over at Bo and recognized the moment for what it was—a good thing. He was a good guy. She wanted her future to have more of this. Quiet, tender moments. With him. In this town that she'd grown to care about. Surrounded by friends she had over for dinner and met for drinks. Forging a family to love.

But before she could have any real future, she had to face the past that was hunting her.

"I've thought about your suggestion of us going to Cold Harbor."

"And?" he asked, wiping crumbs from his hands.

A part of her wanted to see her stepbrother, half sister and new niece. To visit her old friend Savannah. To catch up on all the things that she missed. Even though she had little to share in regard to her own life. "This might sound silly, but what if I make it worse by going back home?" What if doing so antagonized this monster more? Put her family in harm's way?

Bo's knee brushed hers. "It doesn't sound silly. That's why we're going to discuss it first with the team. Weigh the risks versus the reward. See how we cover all the bases." Bo leaned toward her until his face was inches away. "I'm going to protect you until the threat is eliminated, no matter what we have to do to make that happen."

"What about the people I care about there? You can't promise to protect them, too."

His gaze fell. "You're right. Going to Cold Harbor might be the only way to end this, but we won't do anything you're not comfortable with." Looking at her, he came closer still—until his face was all she could see—and cupped her cheek. "You're the client. The choice will be yours."

My decision.

My choice.

Her fear subsided as his words sank in, taking root. Bo was not a careless man. At the church, if she had stayed on the food line, like he had expected, nothing would've happened to her. She trusted him to plan for contingencies. To take her concerns into consideration and keep her from danger.

She missed having this safe space, knowing there was someone she could count on who would be there when she needed them most. Even if this was only a professional obligation for him.

With him sitting so close, his face taking up her full focus, she allowed herself to drink in the sight of him. Such masculine beauty. Nora took in short, shallow breaths, the proximity of him sucking up all the air around her.

His eyes heated, but he didn't move a muscle other than his thumb stroking her cheek. He held her gaze steadily, unwaveringly, like he was waiting for something.

If she leaned her head forward the smallest bit, their lips would touch, but she shuttered her eyes and stayed still.

What do you want your life to look like?

She wanted warmth and connection. Friendship and family. To no longer be trapped and alone. To be safe to finally let herself fall for someone.

Someone like Bo.

But what if she had already fallen?

"Nora," he whispered. "Look at me."

Her gaze lifted to his and she thought she saw the same thing in his eyes that filled every pore in her body. Desire. Need. Longing for something deeper.

Her fingers ached to touch him, and her hand lifted as if beyond her control. She skimmed her fingertips across his cheek and electric heat vibrated through her.

You don't have to be alone. Not tonight.

Then she kissed him, or maybe he kissed her. She wasn't sure.

All she knew for certain was that Bo was touching her and kissing her like he was starving and she was what he craved.

His mouth was hot and possessive. Deepening the slow kiss, he sought her tongue with his own. Sliding her arms around his neck, she drew him closer and everything heated.

She pulled him down onto the sofa and when he pressed his solid, heavy body against her, she moaned in his mouth.

This was better than cookies. Better than anything she'd experienced.

She didn't know her heart could be full of grief and exhilaration, both filling the space at the same moment.

The brutal murders, the senseless loss of life—none of the sorrow left her. The weight still pressed down on her shoulders. But the thrilling rush of this beautiful man touching her, making her ache with need, buoyed her.

She loved the way he tasted, the way he caressed her. Each stroke firm and confident. She loved the way his tongue slid over hers, the way his fingers coiled in her hair.

"You always smell so good," he muttered against her throat.

She kissed him again, lighting up from the compliment. Wrapping her legs around his hips, she yearned for more.

Everything he was doing was perfect. The intensity of his kiss. The searing heat of his hands diving under her sweater. The expert stroke of his fingers making her tingle all over.

But it wasn't enough. Not nearly enough.

Chapter Fourteen

Careful. Go slowly.

He repeated the warning in his mind, but her scent filled his head and her curves filled his palms, kicking his entire body into overdrive. Pent-up desire turned to pulsing need. Yet somehow, he managed to keep a tight hold on the reins of his touch, his kisses slow and gentle, so gentle that it produced an overwhelming ache. Not just a physical ache, but an emotional one, buried so deep inside him that he hadn't even known it existed until this very moment.

The strain from the effort of holding back sent a quiver arrowing straight through him.

He cupped her breasts over her sweater and the shiver that ran through her was impossible to miss. She rocked her pelvis, slow and steady, undulating against him, driving him out of his mind. His jeans tightened painfully in the crotch. He had to do something about the need pounding through him before he combusted.

But the warning sliced through the hormone-fueled fog of his brain again.

Careful. Go slowly.

Bo pulled back. "Nora, what do you want?" he asked, nearly breathless from the hunger tearing at him.

"More."

More. Whispered in that sweet, sultry voice, the word was like an engraved invitation to everything he craved. But he didn't want to mess this up. He needed them both to be clear for her sake.

"More what?" he rasped, his heart thundering in his chest.

"Of this. Kissing. Touching. Everything. But with fewer clothes."

"Fewer?"

"No clothes," she said, then nipped his bottom lip.

He longed to strip off every stitch of clothing from her, but he had more questions. Important ones. Caressing her cheek, he stared into her eyes. "Have you ever been with anyone?"

She stilled and blinked at him. Then shook her head.

"I'd be your first?" he asked hoarsely, needing her to confirm it.

A slow nod. "Is that okay?"

It was and it wasn't. She never had a boyfriend, never allowed herself to get close to anyone, never gave herself a chance to see what she wanted in a lover, in a partner.

An impulsive decision tonight could easily become a painful regret in the morning for her. And he couldn't take advantage of a young client in a stressful situation while she was stuck in his safe house, reliant on him to protect her.

Bo wanted her more than he'd ever wanted any woman, and there had been many. He'd even stopped at the drugstore and while he bought painkillers, he also got condoms since he didn't have any. Always be prepared.

But what he wanted more than her body was her happiness.

Doing this now—rushed, on a whim with no time for her think—was wrong.

She stared at him, waiting for a response. "Please. Don't say no."

He'd made a decision and then she went and said something like that, making him second-guess everything.

No, he chided himself. Even though his body screamed for release, he couldn't do it. "Nora, I—"

A high-pitched frenetic beeping blared in the house, the sound distinct.

The alarm.

Not just the heads-up that a car was headed down the road.

He was off the couch and on his feet. "Someone in the woods tripped the system."

"You mean someone is coming toward the house," she said in a dazed way, sitting up.

"Yeah." He hustled to the office, grabbed the mouse, and the computer monitors sparked to life. With a few clicks, he brought the security system up on the screens and took a look at which sensors had been triggered. Exact same quadrant as yesterday. He followed the flow of activity as one motion-activated detector after another lit up on the screen.

Something or someone was moving in a steady, straight line toward the house, setting off sensors along the way. But it was no animal and no hunter. He was certain of it.

Bo whipped out his phone and sent a text to the IPS group chain.

Activity in the same quadrant. Need backup.

Then he silenced the security system shrieking in the house while keeping it armed so he could track the activity and dialed Tak.

His friend answered on the second ring. "I saw your message. I'll be there in ten minutes. Don't worry about calling E, I'll do it on the way."

"Thanks. I'm going to give you authorization to access my security system remotely, so you can track what I'm seeing. I'll text you a passcode." Bo hung up and got into the system on his phone.

He didn't know if Autumn would get the message about needing backup or if she was already asleep, but he didn't expect her to race out to his place when she lived on the other side of town even if she had seen it. Autumn was a valuable team member, but without tactical training he couldn't use her out here for this.

It was good to have the two other former combat engineers living so close. After they all started working at Ironside Protection Services, they decided to buy properties near each other. Since they were friends beforehand, the best-case scenario was it would be easier to hang out. Worst-case, they could quickly respond if there was an emergency. Their rapid-deployment, wartime-ready nature was ingrained in them.

Always be prepared.

They were each more than capable on their own. But together, they were a formidable force to be reckoned with.

"Is it a person or an animal?" Nora asked as she came up behind him.

"Not sure yet." Bo finished authorizing access for Tak and Eli and texted the code they'd need to get in. Then he hit a couple of different buttons on the keyboard, pulling up the new camera that Tak had installed when he replaced the sensor that had been shot.

Nothing. The screen was pitch black, but the camera was active. What the hell?

Without a doubt, Tak had ensured the camera was functioning properly.

"Why can't we see anything?" Nora asked.

"Good question," he said. "Something's wrong with the lens."

He rewound the footage, going back to a few minutes before the motion activated sensor had been triggered and hit Play on the camera feed.

A clear view of the woods popped up on the screen. Seconds later, a man wearing a ski mask over his face, dressed in all black, entered the periphery of the camera's field of view. He lifted his hand, holding what looked like an air rifle.

Then the screen went black.

"What happened to it?" Nora asked. "Did he shoot it out?"

"No, he didn't destroy the camera. He used something to block out the lens. A paintball would be my guess," Bo said, thinking aloud.

"Why use paint when he could use a bullet?"

"Bullets are loud. Unless you're using a sound suppressor." Which meant this guy wasn't using a silencer. A small comfort in that detail, but not much.

Bo needed to go out there, find him and deal with him personally. Put an end to this nightmare for Nora once and for all.

He refused to simply sit back and allow that brutal monster to slip through his fingers for a third time. *I'm coming for you.*

He jumped out of his chair and hurried toward the front door. "Get your gun."

Nora was right on his heels. "Are we going to see if it's him?"

We? "I don't want you out there. You have to stay in here where you'll be safe."

"Are you leaving me to go out there by yourself?" she asked, fear changing the pitch of her voice. "You shouldn't take him on alone."

A sudden prickling sensation crawled up the back of his neck and made him freeze dead in his tracks. It had nothing to do with his intention to go out in the woods alone. The memory of Nora screaming, bursting through the kitchen doors with blood on her, replayed in his head. How she'd been overcome with terror and fell to her knees in tears, her body racked with sobs.

The blind rage, the fear, the impotence he'd felt in that moment flooded him once more.

The last time that sensor had been activated, he'd left her side to deal with it and that monster had attacked her.

Now, Bo stood there, contemplating doing it again, over activity in the same quadrant of his property.

Coincidences made his inner alarm bell ping because he didn't believe in them.

Maybe this sadistic killer who loved playing games was trying to bait Bo into leaving the house. With the intent of isolating Nora.

But to what end?

His home was secure. The windows were bulletproof. The doors were reinforced with steel and the locks couldn't be picked. They had to be hacked. Which would take time.

Still, the thought of separating from her had his gut tightening with dread.

"No," he said, shaking his head. "I'm not. I'm staying with you."

Relief cascaded over her face, but worry was still heavy in her eyes.

He shoved on his boots and had her do the same. "Get your gun," he ordered as he marched back to office.

They needed to be ready for anything. He opened a drawer, took out extra loaded magazines and shoved them into his pocket.

He sat down in his chair and turned back to his screen.

Sensors had been activated all the way up to his cabin. He checked the four security cameras around the perimeter of the house. Three of them had been blacked out. He toggled over to the feed of the fourth.

Just as the field of view came up on the screen, a paintball hit the camera, covering the lens.

Where are you?

More importantly, what was that devil doing?

If that guy tried cutting power to his house, Bo was prepared. He had a covered generator up on the rooftop deck, making it less visible and harder to sabotage.

Power would be diverted within less than a minute to the house, with only a temporary delay in the security system, but the reboot would take longer. Up to ten minutes. But, with the cameras blacked out, Bo was already blind to what was going on outside.

Sensors in the woods lit back up.

Was the guy on a fishing expedition? Tampering with his cameras and sensors? Testing Bo's security procedures? Or was he still trying to lure Bo from the house, away from Nora?

"Do you smell that?" she asked.

Bo sniffed the air, then went rigid. He did smell it. He looked at the doorway.

Smoke drifted in the hallway. Willowy white streams rolled through the air. The smoke detector screeched, the piercing sound grating on his ears.

"Oh, my God," Nora said, putting a hand to her chest. "He set the house on fire."

A small flame could quickly grow into a raging blaze, spreading unbelievably fast in a matter of seconds. In a few short minutes, the place could be filled with smoke that was just as deadly as the fire itself.

But what part of the house? Is that why he targeted the cameras? Bo spun back to the monitors and checked the system.

A steady seventy-two degrees Fahrenheit in every room of the house. He had an addressable smart multisensor system that registered multiple fire phenomena, such as heat and smoke. It combined inputs from several sensors and processed them using an algorithm built into the circuitry.

The sensors weren't picking up any heat, but according to the system, the smoke originated from the back of the house.

"Bo, we have to get out of here."

He shoved out from behind the desk and hurried toward the back of the house. The white smoke was thick and dense. He took a deeper whiff, noting a sulfury scent. Almost like the odor left in the air after fireworks were set off.

It wasn't fire that he smelled and the smoke was white, not black. Bo should've recognized it sooner. A smoke grenade had been set off. Most likely near the fresh air intake of the HVAC unit.

He swore under his breath. The intake wasn't even necessary for the HVAC to run properly. The only reason he installed the four-inch steel duct that led from the outside to the air return was to pass the home inspection.

Nora coughed, putting an arm up over her mouth and nose. "We have to get out of here."

"It's not a fire!" he said over the blaring alarm, hacking on the smoke as well. They still needed to leave. "He popped a smoke grenade to flush you out of the house since he can't get inside."

Gagging, she stared up at him. "He's out there somewhere waiting. Waiting for me to show myself."

"Yes." It all made sense. Blacking out the cameras. Triggering more sensors in the woods again to draw Bo out. Then that tricky devil was probably going to loop back around and wait for Nora to run out of the house. Panicked. Distracted. Thinking the house was on fire. "Go grab our coats."

"But we can't go out there if he's expecting it. He might have a gun trained on the door, ready to shoot you." She clutched his chest. "We can't."

"We have to." It might not be a fire, but they still needed fresh air. "Trust me. Get our coats," he said tersely, and she took off down the hall.

Bo silenced his phone. He assumed that monster would be perched near the front of the house, but the odds were good that he might be lurking near the back as well. Or even hidden in the woods where he had a view of both doors.

That left them one viable option.

Bo jumped up, snatching the handle in the ceiling for the pull-down stairs that led up to the rooftop deck. He extended the aluminum staircase and locked it in place. Hurrying to the top, he entered the code for the digital lock. He drew his weapon, grabbed the lever, turned it and pushed up on the door.

But it didn't budge. Stuck. Layers of snow and ice must have weighed it down, jamming it.

Nora came to the bottom of the stairs, standing in her coat and holding his. More smoke pumped into the house. He choked, trying not to breathe in too much of the smoke.

He propelled himself up, surging with the momentum,

and threw his shoulder up against the hatch door. Once. Twice. A third time and it gave way. He shoved hard, flipping it open.

A blast of wet wind and snow whooshed down on them. He beckoned to her to follow him.

As Bo climbed out onto the snow-covered deck, freezing wind slapped him. Shivering from the icy cold, he reached down and helped her step up and out.

Slamming the hatch door closed, he took his coat from her and threw it on. Going up to the roof was the best way out of the house, but it also made them visible targets. "Get dow—"

Bullets pinged off the railing in the howling wind. Bo lunged, wrapping his arms around Nora and taking her down to the floor of the deck. More gunfire came from the west. The same side of the shooter's original approach.

Covering her with his body to shield her from the incoming shots, he kept her head down, his arms wrapped around her.

"He's not shooting at me," she said.

Bo realized she was right. This man had murdered five women—that they knew of—and not once had he used a bullet to do it. If he had wanted to shoot Nora, he could've already done so. Whatever his ultimate plan for her, it involved a knife. Not a gun.

"Stay down," he ordered, and she nodded.

He crawled over to the generator that provided some cover while angry flurries whipped around him. Hunkered low, he peered around the side.

Muzzle flashes came from the western tree line near the house.

There he was.

Bo wished he had his Heckler & Koch SL8 rifle. Accurate. Smooth operation. Shot great at a distance. But he was happy to have something. The only problem was that he might not hit the shooter at that range. Bo got down and maneuvered to the side of the generator. Lying in the two-foot-deep snow, he aimed, lining up the sights. He drew in a breath, caressed the trigger, released his breath slowly and took the shot.

Bark spat from a tree and the shadow that had been standing right by it ducked out of sight.

Bo opened fire on the area. Snowy branches fell. Pine needles flew in the air.

A shadow darted between the trees, vanishing into the depths of the woods.

Gunfire erupted deep in the west quadrant. Muzzle flashes, coming from two different directions, converged on one area.

It must've been Tak and Eli zeroing in. But had the gunman been fast enough to make it that deep into the woods?

His phone buzzed with an incoming call. He glanced at the screen. It was Tak.

"Yeah," Bo answered.

"We got him."

Bo peered back into the darkness of the woods. He estimated that it was about four hundred yards from the tree line to the point in the woods where his friends had closed in on the assailant. Less than a quarter of a mile. In a flat-out sprint, in the snow, someone could do it in two minutes. Possibly one and a half. "Are you sure?"

"Eli's got him in zip ties and I just ripped off his ski mask. Mr. Goatee."

"Haul him into the police station. I'll call Logan and Autumn." What role she'd play, he wasn't sure, only that he should update her and ask her to join them. She might be helpful during an interrogation or to support Nora. "We'll meet you there," he said and hung up.

Just to be sure, Bo scanned the trees again for any sign of movement. He climbed to his feet and brushed off the snow from his legs. Scrutinizing the now quiet woods, he waited for relief that didn't come.

Bo helped Nora up. As she dusted the snow from her clothes, he locked the hatch.

Then they used the outdoor ladder along the back of the house. Keeping his weapon drawn and his head on a swivel, he moved quickly to his truck and got her safely inside. He jumped behind the wheel, cranked the engine and set his gun on the console, within easy reach.

Pulling out without incident, he brought up Logan's number in the menu on the dash and called him on Bluetooth. The entire time, the feeling that something was off wouldn't go away.

Chapter Fifteen

"Do you recognize him?" Logan asked Nora.

She stared through the one-way glass at the man handcuffed to a table in the interrogation room. Goatee. Meaty hands. Strong physique. Slight bruises under his eyes. Swollen nose with gauze packed in his nostrils and dressing on the outside. "He might've been the man who attacked me at the church. I can't say for certain because he had a stocking pulled over his head, covering his face. But I do recognize him from one of my open houses. Early November. I remember him because he hovered, but didn't really seem interested in the house."

Logan and Bo exchanged a glance, and in the back of the room, Eli and Tak whispered. She wondered what they were thinking.

"The police can see if his DNA is a match to what they already have from the incident," Bo said, standing beside her. "But do you recognize him from Cold Harbor?"

Nora took another look at him and racked her brain. She'd spent a decade trying not to remember the town and everyone in it, including her family. But Pa, Spencer and Rosa were the ones she'd truly missed and had never been able to forget.

The man in the other room was someone she couldn't

place in her hometown with any certainty. "He has the right build of the guy who attacked me, but I don't know if I've ever seen him in Cold Harbor."

"That's okay," Autumn said, standing on the other side of her. "No one expects you to remember every single person you might have encountered."

Nora was glad that Bo had asked her to come.

"We ran his fingerprints." Logan looked down at a file in his hands. "His name is Louis Ames. Age fifty-two. Has a rap sheet as long as my arm. Petty theft. Shoplifting. Medicaid fraud. Disorderly conduct. Criminal trespassing. Simple assault. All misdemeanors. A repeat offender. But none of his offenses have been violent. He's done several stints in county jails in a hundred-mile radius as well as the state prison three times."

A shudder ran through Nora. "The state prison outside of Cold Harbor."

Autumn put a hand on her shoulder. "Do you want me to get your coat for you?"

They'd left their belongings in the bull pen at Logan's desk. Nora shook her head. "No, thank you." She wasn't shivering from the cold.

"Was Ames free or locked up at the time of the Yuletide murders?" Bo asked.

"Free." Logan glanced back at the file. "He was released two months beforehand."

"It can't just be a coincidence." Bo folded his arms. "Two months before Nora's friends are stabbed to death, that guy is set free from the state prison. Is it located twenty minutes outside of Cold Harbor?" he asked, and Nora nodded. "He's also the one who attacked her at the church, trespassed on my property and shot at us."

"We haven't confirmed that his DNA is a match to that of

her assailant's at the food pantry," Logan pointed out. "With the goatee and the broken nose, he's probably our guy for that. But the only gun Tak and Eli found him carrying was an air rifle filled with paintballs."

"No live ammo on him," Tak said.

"True," Eli agreed, "but that doesn't mean he didn't ditch another gun and ammo in the woods."

"Has Ames been incarcerated at the state prison since then?" Autumn asked.

"Yes." Nodding, Logan flipped through the paperwork. "Two more times. The last was earlier this year. He did six months and was released in March."

"Well, let's go in there and talk to him." Bo gestured at the room on the other side of the glass. "Let's apply a little pressure and see if he cracks."

"When you question him," Autumn said, "refer to Nora and her slain friends as girls. Children. See how he reacts. Whether he naturally talks about her that way himself."

"Why?" Logan asked.

"The killer's desire to play children's games with Nora—Hide and Seek, Sharks and Minnows, Santa Says—it's more than a power dynamic for him. My theory is that he once viewed her that way, as a child, and may still."

"That makes him even more twisted," Bo said. "Wanting to harm children."

"On the note card, the Santa is holding a book of deeds. I believe, in the killer's eyes, Nora is naughty. Maybe because she refuses to play his game. It's something you should test while questioning him."

"All right." Logan headed to the door.

"I need to be in there with you," Bo said. "I know you have a job to do, but so do I. Our goals are aligned, but our priorities aren't the same."

"Yes, they are."

"If that were true," Bo said, "there wouldn't have been a need to send Nora to IPS."

Logan considered it and finally gave a curt nod. "Fine. We'll do it together. Just remember it's being recorded. I know at IPS you only answer to Chance, but I've got a boss."

"I might threaten to push it in there, but don't worry. I'd never do anything that could get you suspended or fired."

"Why does that not make me feel relieved?"

The detective had to follow the strict rule of the law. The same law that prevented him from protecting Nora.

But Bo and the others at IPS would do whatever was necessary to keep her safe.

LOGAN SET A cup of coffee down in front of Louis Ames as they took their seats at the table across from him. He dropped a few packets of creamer and sugar in front of the guy.

"Thanks." Ames tore the packets opened, dumped them all in and stirred the hot coffee with his grimy finger. Then he took long gulps of the hot drink.

"Want to tell me what you were doing out there tonight on private property?" Logan asked.

"Just a prank." Ames shrugged. "No big deal."

"Trespassing and vandalism *is* a big deal," Logan said.

Bo put his forearms on the table and clasped his hands. "Attempted murder is an even bigger deal."

Ames shuttered his gaze and drank more coffee.

No doubt stalling.

"You're looking at some serious time," Logan said. "Did you know you could get fifty years for attempted homicide, with an additional ten years for the use of a deadly weapon?"

"I don't know what you're talking about," Ames snapped.

"Did you find a gun with bullets on me?" The man's beady eyes shifted between them. "I don't think so. You can cut the hogwash. You pigs got nothing on me besides a stupid prank." He drained his cup. "Can I get another coffee and a sandwich this time?"

Logan pulled an evidence bag from his pocket. With a handkerchief, he picked up the cup and dropped it in the bag. "Now we've got your DNA. I'm betting it's going to match the forensic evidence collected after Nora Santana was violently assaulted at the Methodist church yesterday evening. You bled on her when she broke your nose. You made the mistake of picking up a knife during that altercation. When this comes back as a positive match," he said, shaking the bag, "I'm going to charge you with aggravated assault. Then I'm going to put together a case on how you've been stalking Nora Santana. Terrorizing that *girl*."

"Is that how you get your sick kicks? By stalking and terrorizing young girls?" Bo asked.

Ames's beady eyes flared wide with alarm, and they had his full attention now. "No, of course not! Young girl? That woman is a real estate agent. How young could she possibly be?"

"Stalking and terrorizing wasn't enough for you, was it?" Logan took out pictures of Mrs. Moore and Amanda Collins from the file and threw them on the table "Then you murdered her neighbor and coworker. Like you murdered those innocent girls in Cold Harbor ten years ago."

"Hold on!" Ames reared back in his chair. A look of horror wrestled with one of disgust on his face. "I didn't murder anybody! Do you hear me? I may be a thief and a fraud but I'm no killer."

"Unfortunately for you," Bo said, "that's not how any of this looks."

"The public is eager to blame someone for those brutal deaths." Logan crossed his arms over his chest. "I'm happy to throw you to the wolves after your DNA comes back from the assault. And considering your mile-long rap sheet, the judge is not going to go easy on you. Unless…"

Ames gulped. "Unless what?"

Bo leaned forward. "Unless you can give us a better explanation."

"Okay. Listen, I went home one day and found an envelope waiting for me *in* my apartment. On the kitchen counter. It had my name written on it. Inside the envelope was a hundred bucks and a burner phone."

Logan tapped a finger on his notepad. "When was this?"

"Two days before Halloween."

Very precise. "How can you be so sure?" Bo wondered.

"Because it was right after that shooting on Main Street and the person paying me was interested in the woman who was shot but survived. Nora Santana."

Greasy unease slid through Bo's gut. "You got a hundred bucks and a burner. Then what?"

"Then it rang. I answered it. Some guy, or maybe a woman, was on the other end. I couldn't tell for sure because the voice was disguised. By, like, a machine. But I think it was a dude."

"What did the person say?" Bo asked.

"They asked me if I wanted more money. I said, *hell yeah*. They gave me instructions. Every time I did something they asked me to do, I received another envelope with more cash."

"What sort of things?" Bo stared hard at the man. "Start at the beginning and don't leave anything out."

"First it was only following her without getting too close. Once I was told to clean myself up, put on nice clothes and go to an open house she was hosting. The person left something in the envelope that looked like a USB drive but smaller. I was supposed to get her purse, lift her cell phone and insert that drive thingy until it turned green. Then I had to put her phone back without her knowing. That was easy-peasy because she left it sitting on the kitchen counter."

Bo stifled a groan. "Why? What did the USB drive do to her phone?"

Ames shoved a hand through his disheveled hair that looked like it hadn't been washed in weeks. "I don't know. Didn't ask that because I didn't care."

The man after Nora used Ames to surveil her and possibly hack her phone. With some kind of malware?

"Did you ever deliver any notes or gift boxes?" Bo asked.

"No." Ames shook his head. "I was never given anything physical like a gift to give to her or anybody. But I was told to give her a message."

Logan jotted things down even though the interview was being recorded. "A message?"

"Yeah. I was instructed to give her a message when she was at the church."

Bo lifted a palm. "The person on the phone knew in advance that she was going to be at the church?"

"Sure did," Ames said, nodding. "The man, or woman, told me that she was being protected, but that they were going to distract her bodyguard. The big Black guy." Ames looked at Bo. "The bodyguard being you."

Bo gritted his teeth. "Were you told how I'd be distracted?"

"Nope. I asked. He said that I didn't have a need to know. Only that when you weren't focused on the girl. Oh—" Ames straightened "—that's what he always called her. The *girl*. That when you weren't focused on the girl that I had to get to her some kind of way. Not to hurt the girl. Just scare her. Give her the message. He didn't say anything about her hurting me though. She broke my fricking nose."

Logan set his pen down. "Tell us the message."

"He made me memorize it." Closing his eyes, Ames thought for a moment. "Get rid of him and go home alone. If you don't, more will die. More minnows will bleed." He opened his eyes. "That was it. Kind of weird. I had to look up what the heck a minnow was."

A surge of anger rushed through Bo, but he sat back and clenched his hands under the table. "What happened tonight?"

"An air rifle was waiting at my apartment close to dinnertime. Loaded with paintball cartridges. And a map. I got a call and I was told to be at some coordinates in the woods at one in the morning. Sharp. All I had to do was hit the cameras with paint. They were marked on the map. Then I was supposed to go back out the same way I came in."

Bo put a hand flat on the table. "Who was shooting at us?"

"I have no idea."

"You didn't see anyone else?" Logan asked, setting down his pen.

"Nope. No one other than those two fellows who tackled me to the ground, shoved a gun in my face and zip tied me like a hog."

Bo tried to wrap his head around the intricacies of what Ames told them. Setting aside his disappointment and ire that this wasn't their guy and this nightmare wasn't close to being over, he honed in on a gap that needed filling. "You were instructed to follow Nora."

"Yeah, and to keep a log of the things she did, the folks she dealt with, and to pass it along during the calls."

"Why?"

Ames shrugged again. "I told you I don't know."

Bo didn't buy that this man was completely clueless. Ames was a desperate criminal. A criminal smart enough not to get convicted of a felony. Smart enough to be curious. To ask questions. To press for answers even when they were readily given.

"Why didn't this guy follow her himself? And why did he pick you of all people to do it?" Narrowing his eyes, Bo clenched his hand and pounded his fist on the cold metal, making Ames flinch. "And if you tell me that you don't know one more time, we're going to turn off the cameras. The good cop over here is going to leave the room. Then I'm going to ask you again. A different way. One you won't like. I might start by smacking you in your broken nose. And I won't worry about losing my badge because I don't have one."

Eyes big as saucers and sweat beading along his brow, Ames hesitated.

Logan stood. "I guess I'll duck out now."

The chain connected to the handcuffs and table jangled when Ames raised his palms. "Wait. I asked the person why me and refused to work for him until I knew. He told me it was because he knew I needed money and had the right skill set. He knew I'm used to scoping out people and things. Have quick fingers for lifting a phone. Could be mean when necessary. That I'd be willing to deliver some weirdo message and scare that chick."

"And why didn't he follow her himself?"

"I asked that, too. He's not from here. Doesn't live in Bitterroot Falls. Once he let it slip that he had a three-hour drive to get here. He needed someone local. Who could have eyes on her with a phone call."

Cold Harbor was a three-hour drive from Bitterroot Falls.

Every thread of this web led back to Nora's hometown, where this nightmare started.

They needed to go there for answers if they ever wanted to stop this guy.

Chapter Sixteen

Sitting at the conference table, Nora found it hard to believe that the last time she was in this room was three days ago.

In such a short amount of time, she'd endured more than she had over the past three years. She'd lost a neighbor and a colleague at the hands of a relentless serial killer, been attacked by a petty criminal and been smoked out of the safe house.

But she'd also opened herself up to putting her life in someone else's hands. As well as her heart.

She looked up at Bo, who sat across the table from her. Their eyes met, and something in her chest stirred, her thighs tingling, and she felt that irresistible pull toward him—like no one else in the world existed.

Even when they were in a room full of people.

Eli opened the conference room door and stuck his head in the room. "Bo, can I have a word with you in the hall before we start the meeting?"

"Chance is already patched in on speaker. It'll have to wait until afterward."

"If I may," Autumn said, "since you two mentioned that whatever issue you're having is both a personal and professional matter, perhaps it should be discussed with the entire group."

Bo and Eli both averted their gazes, each grumbling some protest.

"This doesn't need to take up the time of the entire group," Bo said.

"There's a client present." Eli shifted his weight, clinging to the door handle. "Bo and I can discuss it later."

Leaning back and angling the chair, Autumn plastered on a plastic expression. "With all due respect, if your discussion involves the client, then it should be had with her present. Does it involve Nora?"

Eli stepped into the room and shut the door. "Yes, it does, but it's a matter of protocol."

Nora stiffened and glanced at Bo for some idea about the problem, but he wouldn't look at her.

"I disagree," Autumn said. "I'm not sure how you're used to operating, but I believe transparency is essential."

Eli shook his head. "It's not your call to make."

"You're right," Chance said over the phone. "It's mine. I agree with Autumn. What's the issue?"

They sat in silence for a long moment that seemed to grow even quieter with each beat of Nora's heart.

"I'm sorry, man. I didn't intend to do it like this." Clasping his hands behind his back like a dutiful soldier—or rather airman—Eli hung his head. "But the fact remains that Bo has gotten intimately involved with Nora. It goes against protocol, could endanger the client and could jeopardize the reputation of IPS."

Nora tried and failed not to squirm in her seat.

"Whatever may have happened between the two of you, was it consensual, Nora?" Autumn asked.

Her cheeks burned like someone had set her face on fire. She could only imagine the embarrassment that Bo must've felt. "Yes. Of course, everything has been consensual. Nothing happened that I didn't encourage or welcome or initiate. Bo has discussed a similar concern with me and frankly, I commend his professionalism and restraint."

The corners of his mouth perked, and she hoped the hint of satisfaction in Bo's expression wasn't her imagination.

"This is my fault." Chance sighed over the phone. "Initially, Bo refused to take this case because of his level of attraction to Nora. I was the one who insisted because she requested him and they already had an established rapport. I thought it was for the best."

"I didn't see a problem with their relationship." Tak picked up his mug of coffee and took a swallow. "Bo offered to be replaced at the hospital and Nora shot down the idea. Quite strongly."

"My professional opinion is that Bo's presence has had a positive effect on Nora's well-being." Autumn spoke to the group but looked at her.

"Regardless, my apologies, Nora," Chance said, "if this has in any way compromised your safety."

"No, no, please. It hasn't. If Bo hadn't agreed to be my bodyguard, I would've run again." Instead of standing her ground and facing this head-on. "This wasn't a mistake. Not for me." When she looked up, Bo was staring at her.

In his eyes, she saw heat and affection and the determination to stay her protector. It wasn't a mistake for him either. She smiled at him, and the grin that spread across his face filled her with warmth.

"Am I the last one to know?" Eli finally took a seat.

Tak nodded. "Always late to the party."

"Moving on to more pressing business," Chance said. "Did you figure out what this guy loaded on her phone?"

"Spyware." Bo sat forward, turning his focus to the speakerphone. "It's allowed him to track her and eavesdrop. Not only on her phone calls, but on any conversation when the phone was nearby."

Since Bo discovered that her phone had been hacked, they'd been careful about anything they said with it around. Before the meeting, he had her leave it in her purse in his office.

"We believe that's how he knew what security measures to expect at Bo's house," Tak said. "Regarding the cameras and sensors."

"And how he tracked her there to begin with," Bo added. "It also explains the convenient timing of him dropping off the package for Nora when the pizza was dropped off. This guy used the delivery as cover."

"Any reason for us to think that he might have picked up on the fact we know about the spyware on her phone?" Chance asked.

"No." Bo shook his head. "Logan is holding the low-level criminal that the killer enlisted to help him orchestrate all this for seventy-two hours before charging him for assault, trespassing and vandalism. After that he'll be moved to the county jail. He won't be talking to anyone."

"We should use this to our advantage," Chance said. "Feed him the information that we want him to know. Flush him out and bait him into a trap. But how?"

"The killer is a three-hour drive away according to Louis Ames," Bo said. "I think the key is to go back to Cold Harbor."

Eli scratched his jaw. "In the report you wrote up after your conversation with Detective Gagliardi, you mentioned that Nora's father, Jamal Banks, is in Bull River. That's a three-hour drive from here, too."

"What does my dad have to do with this?" Nora shifted

in her seat toward him. "The police never suspected him of anything."

"They never investigated him," Eli said gently. "There's also a connection between Banks and Louis Ames."

Anger percolated and she wasn't sure why. "What connection is that?"

"The state prison. Gagliardi told Bo that your dad used to work there as a corrections officer. Granted, it could've been before Ames ever set foot in that prison, but we should reconcile the dates and check out his alibi for the night of the Yuletide murders and the two here in Bitterroot Falls."

The memories she had of her father were all wonderful. Sparse but wonderful. Her mother had always referred to him as a good man. One who had been hurt by their divorce and by her moving on. But there had never been a negative word about him.

"Since you guys are done with the security system upgrade for the other client," Chance said, "Eli, I want you to go to Bull River to check out Banks. Let's do our due diligence on this. Autumn, do you have a profile on this guy?"

"It's not as complete as I'd like, but I'll share what I have thus far. I reached out to a contact of mine in Los Angeles. She's a nose. A sensory evaluator. A professional smeller. I sent her samples of the scent from the box. She identified a series of notes: cashmeran, leather, cloves, pink pepper and juniper. The strange thing is she's not convinced that it's cologne. She thinks it's tobacco. She just received the sample and is still working on it, trying to identify what type and the brand. Also, I scanned the holiday card the killer has been leaving for Nora and did a search for the images. Got a hit on Instagram for the artist who designed and drew the border. She lives in Billings. The woman posted the image of the border in her gallery as part of her portfolio."

Tak sat up like that was the first interesting thing he'd heard. "You contacted her?"

"I did." Autumn nodded. "The person who commissioned her did so through her website. They never actually met. The person provided a description of what he wanted. It reminded her of the European version of Saint Nicholas, where children's deeds are judged. An angel will bring presents or sweets to good kids and Krampus, a devil or monster, comes for the bad ones. She received cash payment in the mail and was told to send the cards to an address in Cold Harbor. To a house on Appleway Road, five blocks from the Howard residence."

Nora's heart skipped a beat. "I don't understand. You found him?"

Autumn frowned. "Not quite. The address was for a Roger Zielinski."

"Mr. Z?" Nora shook her head in confusion. "It can't possibly be him. He's blind. Must be in his late eighties by now."

"He's ninety-two," Autumn said.

"Before I left Cold Harbor, he was already a frail recluse. I can't imagine what condition he's in now."

"Which made him the perfect person to exploit," Bo said. "Easy to go through his mail and take a package without Mr. Zielinski knowing."

"As I told the rest of the team last night, I believe the killer views Nora as a kid. Take his desire to play children's games with her. His usage of Santa. The way he refers to her as a girl. It's most likely because he knew her as one and, I think, once thought of her fondly."

"Fondly," Eli scoffed. "Are you serious? He's trying to kill her."

"He didn't just give her coal. He left sugarplums for her as well. I think his view of her is multifaceted. The note cards being delivered to Roger Zielinski ten years ago does confirm that he lived close by in your neighborhood. That's probably why he disguised his voice. He doesn't want you to recognize him. Not until he's ready for you to know his identity. Probably when he's about to punish you."

It was one thing to think of this man as a faceless, nameless monster, but to realize this was someone she had known well, since she was a child, made her skin crawl. She rubbed her arms to make the feeling go away.

"Are you okay with me continuing?" Autumn asked her. "If you need a break or want to step out of the room—"

"I'm fine. Please, go on."

"Any idea why he might've looked at you or the other girls as naughty?" Autumn asked. "I'm not putting this on you in any way. This could be his demonization of young females for no reason at all, other than the fact you weren't born boys. I just want to make sure we're not missing anything."

"Nothing I can think of. I was a good kid. Never did drugs or drank alcohol. I was well mannered. Got excellent grades. Don't get me wrong—I wasn't perfect. I went through a phase where I cut school sometimes, talked back to my parents, didn't always do my chores. Normal teen stuff." Honestly, she'd started skipping school and sassing her parents as early as seventh grade. Her pa had blamed it on hormones. But after her mom died, she followed all the rules as a way to honor her memory.

"The killer is most likely in Cold Harbor," Autumn said. "That's not to say that we shouldn't completely rule out Banks since the police didn't investigate him and it's not a far drive. However, I think the odds are high that the man we're looking for is white. Not Black. As for age, during the Yuletide murders, he was most likely in his midtwenties to midforties, but I can't narrow it down without knowing if those were his first kills. I do know that he derives gratification from exerting control over Nora. That's why the first game was Santa Says, and it made him so angry when she refused to play. He believes that she deserves to be punished. Perhaps, in his mind, by the devil himself."

"I think we need to go to Cold Harbor as soon as possible to finish this," Bo said. "If we don't, you may never be safe, Nora. But it's your call."

"I'm worried about going back home," Nora admitted. "I don't want to antagonize him. Make things worse. There are people I love who could be targeted."

"Going to Cold Harbor could make him feel backed into a corner." Autumn looked around the room and let that sank in. "It could push him to take a drastic step he wouldn't otherwise consider. On the flip side, the excitement of having her so close again could also cause him to make a mistake. Especially if we make it time-sensitive somehow. Create a sense of urgency in him."

"We need to look at laying a trap there for him," Chance said, "where he feels that he has the upper hand—that he can win. Then we might be able to keep his focus squarely on you, Nora."

His focus and all the danger. She would take on both if it ensured that no one else she cared about was hurt. "It's time I went back home." Faced her demons. Figuratively and literally.

"I'll need backup to cover Nora properly." Propping his elbows on the table, Bo clasped his hands. "I have no doubt that this guy has researched IPS and knows everyone's face. He'll easily spot us."

"Sure, he knows your faces," Chance said. "But not the faces of every IPS agent. We have other offices. Let me talk to Rip. I'm confident I can have some people in Cold Harbor no later than tomorrow morning."

"We can bait him by using the phone he bugged." Autumn rolled a pen between her fingers and looked around as she spoke, like she was thinking out loud. "But I wish there was an organic way to get the town talking about the fact that you're there. The frenzy of chatter around him could push him to slip up."

An idea came to her. "Tomorrow is Sunday. If things are the same as when I lived there, half the town will be at church. I could make an appearance. It would get everyone at the service talking and news will spread faster than wildfire."

"It can work." Bo nodded. "We should go up tonight, which means I'll need backup sooner than the morning. I can ask Winter and Declan. See if they're available. And Jackson might be free. He had to take vacation days to get out of a WITSEC detail so he can attend the engagement party next weekend."

"Who's Jackson?" Nora asked.

"Logan's brother," Bo explained. "He's a US marshal and lives in Missoula."

"Winter is too high-profile," Chance said. "She was the face briefing the media about the mass shooting. If this guy saw Nora during media coverage, I guarantee you that he knows Winter also. Still, check with Declan and I think Jackson is a good idea, too."

"I should go, too," Autumn said. "He'll see me as a target before he thinks of me as a threat. To this guy, women are vulnerable, prey, easy to pick off. But if I'm there, gauging reactions, speaking to people, I might be able to pinpoint who it is."

"Agreed," Chance said. "If we can ID this guy and nail him before we have to use Nora as bait, that would be ideal."

Nora's mouth went dry. She picked up the glass of water and took a sip. This was happening. The possibilities and pitfalls whirled in her head. "So, what's the plan? How do we catch this guy?"

Chapter Seventeen

Glancing in the rearview mirror, Bo checked to see if the car was still behind them. The van was a Ford based on the shape of the frame and pattern of the headlights, but the vehicle stayed too far back in the darkness for him to make out a license plate or see the driver. Getting behind the van proved impossible. Every time Bo had slowed down, so had the other vehicle.

Plenty of other cars were on the road. Yet, that dark-colored van was too similar to the one that had shown up at his house for him to readily dismiss it.

He looked over at Nora. Her head was against the window and she stared outside. Deliberately exposing her to danger set his nerves on edge. There was no other way, and this was better than her running or trying to deal with a cold-blooded murderer on her own. Being by her side, facing this monster together, was crucial for him. As though every moment before this one had led him here. For this purpose. He'd do anything to give her the freedom to live on her terms and without fear.

His mind kept replaying the image of Amanda Collins's body but instead he saw Nora lying there. Bloody and butchered.

Fingers tightening on the steering wheel, he forced the reel of death from his head.

Nora was sitting beside him. Very much alive. He just had to keep her that way.

This was the most important mission of his life. He had to get it right. No matter what.

The plan they had hatched was risky. Jackson and Declan were both available on short notice and would arrive later that evening around the same time as Autumn. Given Nora's concern for her loved ones and Autumn's belief that the killer would likely target a female, the IPS personnel Chance had enlisted—already en route from Spokane— would be assigned to keep a close eye on her sister, Rosa, and old best friend, Savannah. If the killer went after them to use them as leverage against Nora, capable, well-trained individuals would be at the ready to intervene.

So long as everyone did their part without any deviations, they had a good shot at pulling this off and getting justice that was long overdue.

"Are you all right?" he asked without worrying their conversation was being monitored.

Music played and her phone was in the backseat, locked in a dead box. At first, they had considered removing the battery and putting the phone in a Faraday pouch that blocked all signals. But in addition to protecting them from hacking and eavesdropping, it would also prevent the man hunting Nora from tracking her. They couldn't tip their hands.

The next best solution was using the dead box. The GPS and Bluetooth still functioned, but no sound would register while the phone was in there.

Prior to shoving her phone in the box, they had a conversation for the benefit of the eavesdropper that she needed to try to sleep and should stow her gun and phone in the back on the drive.

"I'm nervous," Nora said. "About popping up on my family out of the blue after being gone for a decade. It doesn't feel fair to them. Putting them through that kind of shock and emotional upheaval. In public. I know where Rosa lives. I followed her once. Maybe we could stop there on the way to the B&B and we can get reacquainted privately."

He reached over and took her hand. "We hashed out a solid strategy. To keep everyone safe—Rosa and Savannah—and protect you, too, we have to stick to the plan. It'll be hours before the others arrive. They need time to scope out the lay of the town and get into place discreetly. Seeing anyone tonight jeopardizes the plan."

From the corner of his eye, he glimpsed her nod slowly, like she was considering the situation.

"You're right," she said. "I know. Stick to the plan. I'm sorry."

"Nora, you don't have to apologize for anything."

She took in a big breath and let it out on a shudder. "I think I'll have quite a lot to apologize for to my family."

Provided her pa or brother weren't behind this.

"If I make it through this," she added in a whisper.

"No ifs. *When* you make it through this, you'll be able to see your family whenever you want. As much as you want. You can put this nightmare behind you. Maybe you'll even want to move back to Cold Harbor permanently. The point is you'll be free to choose. To move on." He desperately wanted to give her that. She deserved nothing less than a fresh start.

Nora swallowed hard. "Bitterroot Falls is my home now. I don't want to move on from the town." She interlaced their fingers and squeezed his hand. "Or from you."

His heart swelled at the words and the way she looked at him with such warmth in her eyes. "I'm happy to hear it."

He brought their joined hands to his lips and kissed her knuckles before lowering it to the center console.

He didn't want her to leave, but if that's what she chose to do, he'd have to break his rule about having a long-distance relationship. Maybe even relocate with her.

Whoa. Wanting to follow a woman he'd only known a couple of months, only spent a few days with, sounded absurdly dramatic when Bo was anything but.

Maybe he needed to have his head examined.

At the sign for Cold Harbor, he switched on his signal and took the turnoff. Flicking a gaze up to the rearview mirror, he spotted the van changing lanes and exiting, too. After Bo turned left at the end of the off-ramp and headed to the B&B, he watched the van turn right.

"Thank you, Bo. I've needed you more than I first realized."

"You're welcome," he said brusquely. "But with or without me, you can do this." She just shouldn't have to do it alone.

"I don't know about that."

"Are you kidding me? You've made it ten years without me or anyone else. You were smart enough to learn self-defense, which staved him off in your dorm room, and you defended yourself against a man who was almost twice your size at the church. Sure, you've taken protective measures, keeping others at a distance, but you volunteer all over the place. Giving back to the community when you ask for nothing in return. You have the biggest heart and the bravest spirit." He wanted her generosity and affection for himself, but he wanted to give himself to her in return, to give her everything. As foreign as the feeling was, it made it no less true. "I have no doubt you can do this."

She smiled, so beautiful that it hurt, and something in his chest gave a little tumble.

Then he realized there was nothing wrong with his head.

It was simply falling in line behind the rest of him and leading the way was his heart.

NORA STARED AT herself in the mirror of the room's en suite bathroom, rigid with nerves. When Tak arranged lodging for everyone, he put Jackson, Declan and the IPS agents from Washington at the Roundup Motel in between Cold Harbor and the state prison. While she, Bo and Autumn would stay at the B&B on the edge of town.

It had been unspoken that Bo wasn't going to let Nora out of his sight, which meant one room. No one had questioned it. Tak had reserved the only small suite at the B&B with a sitting area and sofa.

Sharing a room didn't bother her. Wearing a frumpy T-shirt and baggy sweats did.

Given that she had packed a bag with the possibility of running at the forefront of her mind, her choice of clothing had been practical. She'd only thought about survival.

Not seduction.

Last night, Bo had been on the cusp of rejecting her, and after that mortifying group discussion in the office about their *relationship,* she was sure to meet further resistance. It would've been nice to wear something sexy to entice him.

Tipping her head back, she growled in frustration.

The plan the IPS team had created was indeed solid. But past experience taught her that the man after her always managed to be two steps ahead. She hoped everything worked perfectly, but in her gut, she had to account for the unforeseen factor that would invariably rear its ugly head.

By this time tomorrow, she might be dead. As long as they got him, stopped that monster and made him pay for the lives he'd brutally taken, her sacrifice would be worth it.

But she didn't want to die without ever being truly touched, without acting on the desire she felt for Bo. If this was her last night—and she wasn't foolish enough to believe that it might not be—she wanted him to make love to her.

Plain and simple. Yet, getting him to do that might not be.

Leaving the phone on the bathroom floor, where the spy had undoubtedly listened to her shower, she opened the door and stepped into the bedroom. The sofa had been made up with a sheet, blanket and pillow, where he obviously intended to sleep.

The security chain was on, the dead bolt turned and a door stopper was wedged underneath the door.

Turning, she glanced at the bed and her heart started pounding again. Then she saw him standing by the window and her pounding heart fluttered.

Bo was leaning against the wall near the bed, arms folded, peeking out the side of the drawn curtains. He'd changed into navy lounge pants and a charcoal T-shirt that stretched tight across broad shoulders and sculpted muscles.

Her first instinct was to sit on the bed and talk to him. She feared if she did, he'd stay by the wall or retreat to the sofa.

Taking matters into her own hands, she strode over to him, slid her arms around his waist and pressed her cheek to his back, her palms flattening over his rock-hard stomach.

Bo tensed, his muscles flexing. He didn't push her away, which was good.

"Do you see anything outside for us to worry about?" she asked, softly.

"No. I was only checking to be on the safe side. All clear." He turned in her arms and lowered his to fall at his sides. "Big day tomorrow," he said, stopping short and glancing toward the bathroom. "Seeing your family. It's late. You should get some sleep."

She lifted up on the balls of her feet and leaned in to press a tentative kiss to his lips.

Wrapping his hands around her arms, he pushed her back gently.

"I don't want to sleep." She stared at him, searching his face for a hint of desire, but she only saw restraint.

"What do you want?"

"The same thing I asked for last night." She grabbed the hem of her shirt and pulled it over her head. Then she pushed her sweatpants down, stepped out of them and faced him, wearing nothing at all.

On a shudder, a harsh breath tore out of him as his gaze roamed over her.

Resisting the inclination to cover herself, she stood there, letting him take her in.

"You're perfect," he whispered, and she beamed. Then he tilted his head away from her.

Nora slid her palms up his chest and wrapped her arms around his neck, pressing her body against him. "Don't you want me?"

"Yes, of course I do."

"Then what's wrong? Why won't you touch me?"

He sighed and looked at her, his gaze intense and direct. "Why do you want this?"

Why?

A hundred different reasons rushed through her head all at once, like a high-speed train without brakes, but she had no idea where to start. She only knew that mentioning the possibility of dying would not persuade him.

"Rosa and Savvy have full lives. With friends and family and love. With so many things I haven't had because I've been hiding, stuck in limbo. I want more good things to fill up my life." Good things worth fighting for. "Tonight, for a little while, I don't want to feel scared. I want to feel...*good*. When you kiss me, when you hold me, when you touch me, you make me feel good, Bo." Instead of drifting like a ghost, she felt grounded by him. Bo made her *feel*. Sexy. Desired. Smart. Brave. Useful. So many things that she was breathless thinking of it. This incredible man made her feel alive. "Is that wrong?"

"No, it's not." He put his arms around her, holding her close. "What I mean is, do you want this because of a primal urge? Because you want a physical release?" He huffed a heavy breath. "Would you want this if it were someone else here? Eli? Tak? There's no judgment either way. I've had meaningless sex before and I can give you something convenient. Casual. Feel free to use me anytime." He chuckled, the sound halfhearted, and flashed her a soft smile that didn't reach his eyes. "I just need to know. If another man was here protecting you, would you want him to make you feel good?"

Now she laughed, not that it was funny. "You haven't been listening." She caressed his cheek. "No, I don't want just anyone. I want you. I can let my guard down with you. Ever since you took me home from the hospital, I've trusted you. Maybe prematurely, but I felt that I could." Biting her bottom lip, she wondered if she should continue. But she needed him to know. "I want this because I... I'm falling for you," she whispered.

"Yeah?" A real smile this time. "Really?"

She nodded. "But if you only want meaningless and convenient—"

Bo cut her off in what began as a simple kiss. It heated as she opened to him. It became rough and hard and full of need. Shoving a hand in her hair, he groaned in her mouth, his hips doing a slow, grind against her. She curled her fingers in the soft cotton of his shirt, wanting to rip it from his body.

He broke away for a moment, only far enough to whisper against her lips, "I want you. This isn't meaningless or casual for me. Not by a long shot." He crushed his mouth to hers in another scorching kiss.

His arm swept under her legs, tucking her against him. Without breaking the kiss, he carried her to bed. The yearning flaring through her was consuming—a fire that burned deep inside.

Gently, he set her down, pressing his body on top of her. His hips ground against her, a groan rumbling from his chest. She skated her hands down his spine and cupped his backside, drawing the bulge between his legs to her pelvis.

But he shifted, changing position, stoking her frustration and her desire. His lips and hands were everywhere, caressing and kissing.

A moan escaped her, and she reared her head back when he sucked a sensitive nipple into his mouth.

"Too much?" he asked, brushing his lips over the hollow of her throat.

"No. Not nearly enough." She tugged on his shirt, and he helped her take it off him. She gripped his waistband and managed to push his pants to his hips before he grabbed a wrist, stopping her.

"We don't have to go all the way tonight. I can still make you feel good."

Eyes flashing dark and hot, his hand dove between her legs and she gasped, not prepared for the instant pleasure his deliberate touch brought. She writhed helplessly beneath him. His fingers explored her, teasing and stroking while he kissed the valley between her breasts. Whimpering, she bucked her hips up, rubbing against his palm, needing friction, wanting more of him. All of him.

"Please." Her breath hitched in her throat. "Please, Bo."

"Please, what?" he murmured across her breast, his tongue tickling her skin. "What do you want?"

"You. I want to…"

His thumb hit a hot button of nerves and sensation detonated inside her. Shuddering, she cried out against the wave of pleasure that was swift and sharp.

Turning on his side, he held her, kissing her throat and running his nose along her skin up to her jaw. "We can stop. I can do other things. We have options." The hard length of his arousal pressed against her thigh, and she ached for so much more. "I just need to know how far you want to go."

Rolling over to face him, she stared in his eyes, slipped her hands down his pants, cupped him, and he groaned. "All. The. Way."

A grin tugged at his mouth, and he was off the bed in a flash. Her heart and body throbbed in anticipation. He closed the bathroom door, turned on music, dug in his overnight bag and came back to bed with a box of condoms.

Laughing, they pulled back the covers and climbed under the sheets. He settled between her legs and looked down at her.

There was desire in his eyes, but also something much deeper.

"I need to get this out now. Beforehand. I don't want you to think it's because we made love."

He took a breath like he was gearing up to say something serious. If he hadn't grabbed the condoms, she would've been certain another rejection was coming her way.

"Nora, you're special to me. I've never felt so strongly about anyone. We have a connection. One I need to hold on to. One I don't want to live without." Then he smiled at her softly, full of affection, and that single look mended the fractured pieces of her heart.

Chapter Eighteen

At eleven o'clock on Sunday morning, Bo and Nora watched the church doors as they waited for the ten o'clock service to finally end. Once it did, people would congregate outside, and they would make their move.

He didn't care that they'd been parked on the far side of the lot for thirty minutes. Or that the service had run longer than expected.

They were ready to rock and roll. The players on his team were in place. Autumn was in her SUV beside them. Declan and two other IPS agents were somewhere in the vicinity, keeping a low profile, observing. Jackson was at the B&B where he'd camp out as backup. Bo had given Detective Gagliardi a heads-up about their little op since it was in her backyard and asked her to keep quiet about it. She agreed, provided they include her once it was time to reel the killer in.

Nora wore the necklace Bo had given her. A tracking device with audio capability was hidden inside the pendant. He was taking no chances.

Since her stalker knew about her Beretta, and would certainly plan for it, Bo had given her a pocketknife and a Ruger LCP. Lightweight at less than ten ounces and compact with a length of only five inches, the backup gun was easy to conceal in the holster around her ankle. Despite the weapon's small size, it held seven rounds and packed a powerful punch.

He was even prepared to trade out his blue Toyota Tacoma for an all-wheel drive SUV.

With contingencies mapped out and every base covered, he allowed himself a few minutes to simply breathe. Just until those church doors opened.

He allowed two words to repeat in his head.

Mine.

She's mine.

He glanced over at Nora sitting in the passenger's seat and couldn't believe his luck. She was so beautiful. Kind yet tough. Caring and generous. As if all of that weren't enough, when they'd made love last night, she'd been perfect. Better than any fantasy. Tight and hot and just as hungry for him as he'd been for her. Like she'd been made for him.

He'd brought her to the brink and pushed her over the edge. With his fingers. With his mouth. Joining as one as he'd taken her, made love to her, and she had taken him, eyes closed, head thrown back, spasming around him until he had collapsed, boneless, burying his face in her hair.

It was pure pleasure, but it had gone deeper than the physical. It was proof that this thing between them was right.

Mine.

She was his and he was hers. For the first time, he'd found someone worth fighting for in every way.

Her eyes lifted, meeting his, and she smiled at him, but then she looked back at the church and the joy on her face faded.

Something was wrong.

He didn't expect her to be happy to involve her family in their plan, but she'd been acting differently since they left the B&B. Off somehow. Like a wall had gone up between them.

"Nervous?" he asked, not able to voice the real question running through his head because her phone was in her purse and the spyware was active.

She only nodded.

The church doors swung open, redirecting his attention across the parking lot.

Bo had gone over the Facebook pages of Nora's family and friends and some of the townsfolk who had a social media presence, making it easy to spot them as they emerged from the church.

People began filing out. Keith Graham and his wife, Sandy, were the first ones to shake the minister's hand. The former mayor was ten years older than his wife, though the age gap looked larger. Speaking to the minister, they wore amiable expressions, but when they went down the stairs to the walkway, tension between them became apparent, and their conversation ceased.

The temperature was mild, in the high forties, and there wasn't much wind. No reason why folks wouldn't stand around and socialize a bit.

Once a handful of individuals had made their way to the bottom of the stairs, Sandy Graham peeled away from her husband, leaving him alone, and eagerly chatted with others. The older man interlaced his gloved hands and stood there as though this was routine.

Spencer waltzed out of the church, carrying a toddler with a head full of dark ringlets. Savvy was by his side.

In the passenger's seat, Nora stiffened, wringing her hands.

As Spencer and Savvy spoke with the minister, Savvy's father, Terry, limped over to join them. Graying with a weathered face, Terry used a sturdy wood cane with a brass embossed collar. The handle was slightly curved at the end, making it easy to hook on a table or the crook of one's elbow. Slowly, he hobbled behind Spencer and Savvy, needing to take the stairs one step at a time.

In one of Savvy's online posts, she'd mentioned her brother Dylan's promotion to foreman in the coal mine and how they'd be able to help their father, who was scraping by on his disability checks.

Each vile gift box that Nora received contained a piece of coal. It occurred to Bo that the police had never questioned Dylan or any of the people at the party he supposedly attended without his good friend Spencer. Even if Dylan had gone, how simple would it have been to sneak out and blend back in later?

Where was Dylan now? Bo didn't spot him in the crowd. A no-show?

Rosa sauntered outside and Nora leaned forward, putting her hands on the dash. The two women bore a distinct resemblance. They had the same heart-shaped face and amber-colored eyes. The younger sister was shorter than Nora's five-foot-seven-inch frame—even with chunky winter boots—and had dark straight hair rather than wild curls.

The man with his arm around her shoulders was the new husband who Nora had never met. Behind them, Frank Howard hovered. Nora's pa looked uncomfortable for a moment, sweeping a hand through his silvered ebony hair. When it was his turn to step in front of the minister, he looked ready to shake his hand and move along.

"Okay." Bo turned to Nora. "This is it."

She sat there, quiet, gazing across the lot at the church.

"Don't you want to meet Rosa's husband? Hold your niece? See your family?" he asked. She still didn't respond.

"Remember why we're here. So you can find answers. This is the only way."

"This isn't the only way," she snapped.

What was she doing?

Autumn got out of her car, came up to the driver's side window and held her hands out, silently asking the same question.

"If we're going to do this," Bo said, "we have ten minutes before they disperse and go home."

"I want to leave. Drive."

PULLING HER WOOL coat closed, Autumn tugged the purple scarf wrapped around her neck higher to cover her chin. She knocked on the window and waited.

Shoulders sagging, Nora picked up Bo's cell phone and gestured for him to unlock it. He did. She opened his texts and started a new message but didn't select a recipient.

Send Autumn back to Bitterroot. She's a friend. Makes her vulnerable. A liability. Now! Please!

What about going to the church? Speaking to your family? What happened to the plan? he replied.

Nora pointed to her message. "You and Autumn think I should be here in Cold Harbor. This isn't the way I want to handle things. I don't like the pressure. From either of you." Again, she gestured to the message.

Scrubbing a hand over his jaw, Bo turned to the window. Rolled it down. "I want you to go back to the office. You're not needed here," he said.

"What changed?" she asked, carefully.

Quickly, he weighed what to say. "I don't answer to you. It's the other way around. Go back to Bitterroot Falls."

Autumn drew her brows together in confusion. *Really leave?* she mouthed.

He nodded, once.

Pursing her lips together, Autumn spun on her heel, got into her car and drove off.

"Satisfied?" Rolling up the window, Bo shifted to Nora and took his phone from her. "Pressure cut in half."

He typed a message.

What are you doing? Stick to the plan.

Holding the phone low, he showed her the screen.

She read it and looked up at him. "I'm not satisfied. I don't want the pressure cut in half. I want it down to zero. Completely eliminated. Take me back to the B&B."

Narrowing his eyes, he stared at her, trying to pull an answer from her.

She snatched the phone from his hand, shoved it into the cup holder and faced forward. "Please. Take me."

"Are you sure?"

"I'm positive that I don't want to go out there and risk getting anyone else hurt." She glanced at him. "Your way isn't the only way. Trust me," she said, her eyes imploring him.

Bo threw the gear of his truck in Drive, wheeled out of the lot and hit the main road.

He hated this. Not being able to talk freely with her to understand what she was thinking. Find out why she was deviating from a plan after they had gone through painstaking efforts to make it work.

They drove in silence. Ten minutes without a word exchanged until he pulled up in front of the B&B.

Reaching over, he took her hand. He wasn't sure in what direction her changes were going. The best thing he could do was follow her lead. "Nora, you're an IPS client, first and foremost. But you're also my friend." Such a tame word that didn't scratch the true surface of what she meant to him. "I care about you and want to help you. I thought reconnecting with your family—getting questions answered, finding out what you've missed in their lives—would get you closer to what you ultimately want."

"It isn't necessary to drag my family into this. I want to see them, which makes me selfish. Last night you gave me something special that I needed. Thank you," she said, giving his hand a small squeeze before snatching it free of his grip. She looked out the window. "But it was simply sex. Nothing more. We shouldn't confuse hormones with something else. It'll only make this harder."

"What harder?" he asked, trying to decide how much of this they'd discussed in advance and how much of it was coming from a different place he was struggling to grasp.

"You and Autumn think you know what's best for me, but you don't. I never should've come to you and IPS." Her tone was deadly serious. "I never should have come back to Cold Harbor. It was a mistake. The only thing I can do is something I should've done four days ago. *Run*. Wipe away everything that's Nora Santana. My business. My charity work. Leave it all behind. My house. My car. My phone. Disappear and stay gone for good. Start over somewhere else as someone else."

Some elements he recognized, but the rest of what she was saying was sending him into a tailspin. "And your family?"

"Seeing my family will only hurt them. They don't want me to dig up painful memories that they'd rather forget. I have to let them go." Her jaw trembled, cheek quivering, and she pressed her lips together in a hard line. "The same way I have to let *you* go."

Bo reeled back in his seat. "Don't do this." *Don't go rogue.*

"This is the only way. I purchased an airline ticket. Later tonight, I'll fly out of Missoula. I don't want you to follow me. Not into the B&B and not to the airport."

"You can't be serious. I have to go inside to get my stuff. We can sit down and talk this through."

"I'll ask the owner of the bed and breakfast to mail you your things. I'll pay for it. Just get out of here and go back to your life."

"Nora, I can't leave you like this. I won't."

"You have to. Because I'm a bad omen. Anyone who gets close to me dies and I don't want that for you." Sucking in a deep breath, she looked at him, meeting his gaze, and held it. "Bo, you're fired. I don't want anything else to do with IPS." Tears welled in her eyes but she hiked her chin up. "If you don't leave me alone, I'll call the police. I hope you can understand this is for the best." She hopped out of the truck and slammed the door shut behind her.

NORA MARCHED UP the B&B porch steps without a single glance back at Bo. She strode through the foyer and caught sight of a man in the front sitting room. Blond and handsome, he looked like a younger, broodier version of Logan. Her only guess was that he was Jackson.

He made no eye contact with her, and she did her best to minimize any overt focus on him.

She hurried up to the third floor, went into the small suite and locked the door.

Plunking down on the bed, she wrung her hands. One thing she'd learned over the years of running and starting a new life was that the best lies were half-truths. Every word about her family had come from the pain in her heart.

She worried her presence would only resurrect ugly memories of death. That she'd stir up unwelcome emotions. That her presence would cause more harm than good. Endangering them wasn't an option. She wasn't going to play games with their lives for the sake of exciting a despicable killer.

Nora also wasn't willing to put Autumn in harm's way. They'd become friends and Nora wasn't going to paint a bull's-eye on the back of anyone she cared about. Not even Bo.

There was no need. None whatsoever.

The man stalking her was spying on her, and he already knew she was in Cold Harbor. The plan had been to spend the day with her family. Try to get some answers and piece together this deadly puzzle.

Then fight with Bo. Mention leaving her hometown and Montana for good in the morning—though she'd pushed up that timeline by twelve hours. The IPS team had stressed the importance of creating a sense of urgency. To her, this was a job well done.

Next, she needed to go back to the bed and breakfast alone.

And wait.

Wait for that monster to take the bait and show himself.

In the event he didn't come for her today, where this could be finished one way or another, she had told Bo another hard truth.

Running might be her only choice to protect everyone else. Otherwise, there was nothing to stop him taking more lives to coerce her into playing one of his games. So, she had purchased an airline ticket from Missoula to Seattle. From there, she'd take a ferry to Alaska. Reinvent herself in the last frontier. Go off the grid if necessary. That was surely the perfect place to do it.

Abandoning the life that she'd started building in Bitterroot Falls and walking away from Bo would devastate her.

But she'd make any sacrifice for the people she loved. They'd only been together a few days, shared one passionate night, yet it felt like she'd known him for years. Every time she thought of him, she saw him as a part of the future life she wanted.

She took a deep breath, held it and exhaled.

For now, she would follow the IPS plan. With modifications.

It was impossible to know how long she would be waiting. The last departure out of the Missoula airport was eight o'clock tonight. With an hour and a half drive to get there, plus time to check in, if the man who'd been obsessed with her for a decade was coming for her, he'd have to make a move no later than 5:00 p.m.

The only question was, did he need the cover of darkness or was he bold enough to maneuver in the light of day?

In less than three hours, she had her answer when her cell phone rang. A random number she didn't recognize.

This was it.

The last game she was ever going to play with him.

Winner takes it all.

Chapter Nineteen

Bo sat behind the wheel of a Subaru SUV with tinted windows that he had exchanged with Tak, who had taken his truck.

Parked on the side street of the intersection that faced the B&B, he stayed seated low, wearing shades and a cowboy hat because it blended in more than a ball cap. In one ear he had comms to speak with the team. An earbud was in the other, connected to his laptop, which he used to monitor the device hidden in Nora's necklace.

Declan and Detective Gagliardi were stationed on the road parallel to the one the bed and breakfast was on, and Jackson was inside the house, where he could cover both the front and back entrance.

Bo only wished he'd been able to have a candid conversation with Nora before they'd separated. The things she'd said to him hadn't all been for the sake of a pretense. The tears in her eyes had been real.

Did she really intend to leave? Disappear and start over somewhere new without him?

A cell phone rang. Not his.

Dropping his gaze to the laptop screen, he saw that it was Nora's.

"Look alive," he said over comms. "She's got action."

Bo turned up the volume and prayed she put the call on speaker so he could hear both ends of the conversation.

"Hello," she answered.

"Sweet Nora." The voice was digitized and crystal clear through the phone's speaker.

If Bo could've kissed her, he would have.

"You came home," the voice said, "and you got rid of him. Good girl."

Clenching a fist, Bo scanned the area for any other parked cars that hadn't been there earlier, any vehicles cruising or anyone lurking.

"Ready to finish playing?" the voice asked.

"What do I get if I am?"

"Peace of mind. I won't harm anyone else you care about. Not if you play. Are you ready?"

A moment of hesitation. "Yes," she said.

"Santa says, go out the back door of the bed and breakfast. Beyond the yard, there's a forest. Take the trail on foot and don't stop until I tell you. No coat. No purse. No gun. If you're followed, I'll know and there will be fatal consequences for someone you care about. If you hang up, there will be consequences. If you stop before I say so, you won't make it in time."

"In time for what?" Tension raised the pitch of her voice.

"To finish this round of Santa Says. Then we'll have to play a new game. A very bloody game."

"No, please. Don't hurt anyone else. I'll do it."

"Good girl. Santa says, run, Nora. Go now."

Bo tapped his earpiece. "Jackson, hang back and give her space. Three minutes. Four tops."

"I might lose her if I do."

Bo swore, his gut burning over having to make a choice. Over wanting to pick her over everyone else when she would beg him to choose differently. "We risk the chance of him seeing you and someone else paying the price with their life." Nora would never forgive herself or him. Maybe he could still protect her without jeopardizing anyone else. "We'll track her via GPS and tail her at a distance by car." He was already moving, readying to drive the perimeter of the forest until he came across a road that cut through. At the same time, he was trying to bring up a map.

"She's out the back door," the youngest Powell said. "Those woods stretch for miles. I don't know where they could lead or if you'll be able to reach her destination by car. And she's fast. Really, really fast."

"The woods lead to a lake, the quarry and coal mines," Gagliardi said, coming over comms. "If she steps foot inside those mines, kiss your GPS coverage good-bye. You won't be able to track her, and you may never find her. Not alive, anyway."

By not following her on foot, he might be trading her life to save someone else's.

Nora might hate herself and hate him, too, if there was more innocent blood shed because he made the wrong choice. But he'd take her hatred over her death. The gamble of her being led or dragged into the coal mine was too great.

Bo would sooner play Russian roulette with his own life. He couldn't bear it if he lost her. *Choosing you, Nora, can't be wrong.*

"Follow her, Jackson. Just try to stay out of sight."

KEEP GOING. *Don't slow down. Don't stop!*

Nora was gasping for air, panting, her mind whirling as she tried to anticipate what surprise might come next. With no time to strategize, all she could do was run.

Her thoughts were racing as she kept sprinting, even as

her body protested. Her shoulder ached now, a throb that spread down to her hand. She tucked her left arm, pressing it against her torso, and only pumped with her right arm to boost her momentum.

A cold wind whipped through the snow-covered trees, cutting through her and slapping her face. She shivered so badly, she had difficulty thinking straight. Perhaps that was the point. To have her too cold, too tired, and in too much pain to fight back.

One thing at a time. Put one foot in front of the other. One move, then a countermove.

She just had to run until he told her to stop. Her legs were strong, and so were her lungs. They would carry her through this. Ignoring the bite of pain in her shoulder, she stayed on the trail as he instructed.

"Go toward the trees with the yellow ribbons tied around the trunks," the voice said.

Past a cluster of evergreens, she spotted the ribbons. Silky streamers bright as the sun billowing in the wind. More than a quarter of a mile away.

Her lungs were on fire, but she could do it.

CRANKING THE WHEEL HARD, Bo made a right turn that had the tires screeching as he left the paved road and hit the dirt trail that ran through the forest.

A glance at the laptop screen told him he was going the correct way. She was headed straight for the road and would hit it farther down.

It occurred to him that someone else might be on the road. A road that led to the coal mines. His heart skipped a beat. The man they were after might be there waiting to intercept her. And if he got her into a car—

Bo smothered the thought. He didn't want to go there.

Nora understood the danger of being moved to another location. Being forced to run wasn't much better. But there was a big difference between traveling on foot and by car. The distance could grow exponentially within a matter of minutes. Seconds.

What if Bo was spotted on the road? Would that endanger her? Would she suffer consequences?

Slowing down, he triangulated, looking at where he was in relation to her current position and where she was headed. He could reach her on foot from here if he ran quickly, but he'd have to leave his laptop and rely on the others to be his eyes and ears, updating him on her progress. He couldn't afford to miss her. Not by a second.

"I'm going on foot the rest of the way," Bo said, pulling over as far off the road as possible. "I don't want the car to be seen." He hopped out of the SUV and shut the door quietly, not wanting to make any noise that would draw attention.

"Jackson, what's your status? Do you have eyes on Nora?" Bo left the well-worn path, ducked in between trees and took off deeper into the woods.

"Negative." Jackson huffed, sounding winded. "But I see the yellow ribbons."

Look for the yellow ribbons, Bo reminded himself.

KEEP MOVING! She groaned through the discomfort of her shoulder and the burn in her chest. *Almost there!*

One of the yellow ribbons was almost within reach. But she still didn't have a plan. She had to outsmart him, outmaneuver him.

Somehow.

Overpowering him was impossible at this point. Inside, she was shredded. Totally spent. She used what little she had left in the tank to push onward to a tree with a yellow ribbon.

"Stop!" the voice commanded

Nora halted. Gasping, she tipped her head back and raked in as much air as possible.

"Walk to the center of the trail."

Heart on the verge of bursting from her chest, she slogged forward like he demanded.

"Stop."

She stood still, trying to recover. The physical toll of sprinting in the cold with no coat on was too much, sapping her mentally, too.

Looking around, she spotted a van parked a hundred yards down the trail. Was he inside it?

"Lift your sweater up and turn around," the voice said, "so that I can be sure you're not carrying a weapon."

Nora grabbed the hem of her sweater and pulled it up, stopping short of exposing her bra, and spun in a full circle.

"Drop the phone."

She released it from her grasp, letting it hit the cold ground.

Then someone wearing a ski mask stepped out from behind a tree in the woods on the other side of the trail. He held up a gun, aimed it at her and approached her slowly.

Panic seized her roiling gut as she raised both palms.

Once he reached the trail, he dug into his pocket and took out a pair of flex cuffs—disposable zip tie handcuffs—and tossed them at her feet. "Put them on," he said, still using the digitized voice, "and tighten them with your teeth."

Not happening. "I don't think so." She could finally breathe again.

He reached toward his back, pulled something from under his black sweater and held it out for her to see.

A purple cashmere scarf.

Autumn's.

"If you don't, our game ends, and I'll play a different one with your friend. The psychologist."

Terror sliced her down to her core. Not for herself, but for Autumn.

Squeezing her eyes shut a second, Nora shook her head. This monster kept besting her. Outwitting her at every turn. She'd sensed that Autumn might be in danger and she'd been right.

Why did Nora agree to let her come to Cold Harbor in the first place?

Now, he had her. A good, kind woman who had only tried to help her through this mess.

Nora wanted to scream, attack this sick animal and beat him to a pulp. But what had he done to Autumn?

"Is she hurt?" Nora asked.

"I left her undamaged. For now. If you want her to stay that way, put on the cuffs."

Clenching her jaw to keep her teeth from chattering, Nora swallowed the hot bitterness that filled her mouth. She bent down, picked up the cuffs and slipped them on her wrists.

"Tighten them."

She yanked each strap with her teeth until the plastic straps tightened, digging into her skin. "Show me your face. Some part of you wants me to know who you are and why you're punishing me. So, let me see who you are."

He stepped closer until he was within arm's reach. Sticking his hand under the mask, he peeled off the voice digitizer that had been affixed to his throat and tossed it down. Then, slowly, he pulled off the mask.

Nora rocked back on her heels, her mouth falling open in disbelief. "You?"

Bo's PHONE BUZZED. Incoming call over comms. Whoever it was wanted to speak to the entire team. Tapping the earpiece twice to connect, he didn't slow.

"It's me," Autumn said. "I'm here."

"Where?" He wanted to ask if she was back in Bitterroot Falls, but he saved his breath, needing it for the run.

"Cold Harbor. I never left."

If he had the lung capacity to curse without slowing down, he would've. The one thing Nora had wanted was for Autumn to leave and stay safe. Instead, she had defied an order.

"Why not?" Declan said, asking the question that was on the tip of Bo's tongue. "This killer only targets women. Women close to Nora. That makes you a potential target."

"Stop. I'm fine. I stayed to talk to Rosa and Savvy. I had a feeling that they might know more than they realized. Questions about the case led nowhere. A dead end. I showed them the note card and they'd never seen the drawings. But I brought a sample of the seat cushion from Nora's car that still had that smell of cologne or tobacco trapped in it."

"And?" Bo managed to say.

Spotting yellow streamers up ahead in the distance, he slowed down. He was too close now to go tramping along.

"Savvy recognized it. Pipe tobacco."

"Whose?" Three of them asked at once.

"Terry Watts."

NORA WAS REELING in terrified shock.

"Hands up. High in the air," Mr. Watts said, and she raised them.

Stepping even closer, he patted her down, starting with her breasts.

Her heart sank. Bo had given her extra weapons to defend herself and he was about to find them.

The pocketknife first. He pulled it from her pocket.

Her only hope now was that he was tracking her.

Terry Watts tsked at her like she was a child or a dog and tossed the blade to the ground. "Naughty, naughty, Nora."

"Why are you doing this?"

"Twelve stab wounds. The card with Santa and Krampus." He stroked down one of her legs. "You really don't remember, do you?"

"Remember what?"

Down the other leg. His hand stopped on the gun holstered around her ankle. "The lives you destroyed." With his gun aimed at her midsection, he yanked up her pant leg and unstrapped the holster. He tossed it back in the woods. "Walk to the van," he said, gesturing for her to move.

She lowered her hands. Taking her time, giving Bo a chance to reach her, she took slow, deliberate steps. "What are you talking about?"

"It was the week before Christmas break. That day you skipped school along with Jessica, Alice and Dana. You went back to your house. Saw your Pa and—"

"My mom." They were being intimate with the bedroom door open, thinking no one was home because the kids were supposed to be at school. Nora had only glimpsed them before skedaddling out of the house with the others. A few days later, her mother yelled at her about a skirt she was wearing. How short it was—almost indecent. Nora snapped, said things she regretted, told her mom that she wasn't going to grow up to be *loose*. Would never bring boys to the house in the middle of the day to have sex the way her mom and pa had. Nora had been a silly, rude twelve-year-old to speak that way.

Twelve. They had all been twelve. Her, Jessica, Alice and Dana.

Twelve stab wounds.

"No. It wasn't your mother. It was my wife. Peggy. Your mom didn't know about the affair. Neither did I. Not until you told her inadvertently." He shoved the gun in her face. "You caused that car accident, you know. We all went out to dinner. Luisa had been tense, acting weird. It wasn't until we all got in the car and Peggy and Frank sat in the back that she brought it up. That you four, rotten twelve-year-old girls had played hooky from school and caught them. Frank and I started arguing. Luisa got distracted. Only for a split second. For the wrong second. And hit that truck."

"Oh, my God." Nora lurched forward, sick to her stomach. "I never had any idea."

"Your pa didn't want you to know. Didn't want you to carry that on your shoulders. But it's your burden to bear." He stopped as they reached the van. "That argument, that accident, changed my life. I didn't think I'd ever fully recover. I did. But then Peggy got sick and needed full-time care. I pretended that I was still injured so I could look after her. Do you know what that's like? To love someone so much and to hate them for betraying you, but to be stuck tending to them, watching them slowly wither away?"

Nora swallowed around the lump in her throat. "I'm so sorry, Mr. Watts."

"It's too late for apologies. You need to pay for what you did."

"I didn't know. If I had, I never would have said anything to my mom."

"If only you and Alice and Jessica and Dana had been good girls." Mr. Watts reached behind his back again and this time his hand came up with a boning knife. "If only you had gone to school that day like you were supposed to." He lowered the gun in his right hand and raised the knife in his left. "Then you never would have found out. Luisa and I wouldn't have either. Our lives wouldn't have been destroyed. Your mother would still be alive. And I could have tended to Peggy for four years without hating her. You wretched girl!"

Nora kicked his leg, hoping that it wasn't fully healed, and interlocked her fingers. She batted his arm with her clasped hands, knocking him into the side of the van. She whirled around and sprinted toward a tree, praying she could duck behind it for cover before he took aim and squeezed the trigger.

A gunshot blasted the air, chilling her down to the marrow in her bones. She froze, waiting for the pain. But no agony followed.

Bo darted out of the woods and rushed toward her. Holding out his arms, she ran to him. It wasn't until he held her that she realized she was shivering.

She looked over her shoulder.

Terry Watts was on the ground, eyes open, dead.

Jackson Powell burst from the woods and hurried to the body. He knelt down and checked for a pulse, then picked up his gun.

"It's over," Bo said, brushing his lips across her forehead. "He's never going to hurt you, or anyone else, ever again."

Chapter Twenty

Six days later...

They were all gathered at Chance and Winter's house. The luxury ranch home was enormous, with eye-catching amenities and high-end decor that would exceed any real estate agent's expectations. Set on one thousand pristine acres, the swanky retreat was the perfect spot for Summer Stratton and Logan Powell's engagement party.

Sitting on Bo's lap on the sofa, Nora leaned against him as he slid his arms around her, holding her close. The spacious living room was packed with Strattons and Powells, most from out of town, as well as friends and plenty of people from Bitterroot Falls.

Nora soaked in the festive atmosphere and, to her surprise, the holiday spirit, too. With Christmas less than a week away, the house was decked out in decorations and string lights. Presents were piled under the tree. Lively music played in the background while everyone chatted, ate and danced. A spirited debate continued over where to hold the nuptials. The Powells wanted Wyoming, on their large ranch, where they had dreamed all their children would be married. The Strattons wanted Texas, where they had lots of relatives who wanted to attend. The newly engaged couple wanted to stay out of it, choosing to dance and kiss.

The love-fueled discussion reminded Nora what it was like for things to be normal, to be around family. It seemed hard to believe that just six short days ago, she had finally faced her demons and almost died. If not for Bo and Jackson racing to her aid, she would be dead. The incredible man who was holding her now had taken the shot that saved her.

So much had come to light with Terry Watts finally paying for what he had done. Answers to her questions had surfaced. All these years, her pa had been hiding the fact that she had discovered his affair. He'd been plagued with such shame at having cheated on her mother. A short-lived dalliance during a difficult time in their marriage. One he regretted so much he'd tried to drown it in booze. But he had never wanted her to feel responsible for any of the fallout. Especially not for the horrible accident that had killed her mother.

On the night of the Yuletide murders, Spencer had lied to the police about being home. Instead of watching movies in his room or going to the party with Dylan, he had been with Savvy. He'd had a crush on her, way back then, but knew he had to wait until she was older to act on his feelings. However, when he found out she had the flu, he'd brought her soup and watched a movie in her room to keep her company, not caring if he got sick.

They later connected the dots that years ago, in Cold Harbor, Terry had arrested Ames. Terry must have seen Ames again in Bitterroot Falls and decided to use the ex-convict to help carry out his plan.

A deadly plan that had nearly succeeded.

Renewed relief washed over Nora as she tightened her arm around Bo and pressed her cheek to his.

No more living in fear. No more running. No more hiding. No more pushing people away to protect them.

It was still surreal.

"You want to dance?" Bo asked with a smile that made her heart flutter.

"Sure."

They rose together. He set her down on her feet and twirled her while keeping a steady hand on her so that she didn't fall.

She wrapped her arms around his neck and his hands went to her waist to pull her tight to him. Leaning down, he kissed her softly and she tingled. Bo understood her and accepted her. After fighting to survive for so long, suppressing her opinions and desires in order to blend in, he encouraged her to stand out, to tell him what she wanted even if it caused an argument. He made her believe that no matter what, they could work it out.

Every night, whether they were at his house or hers, they talked for hours about everything. Made love and talked some more. They were healing each other, and Nora felt herself changing as she opened up about the things she kept locked away inside her.

Bo pulled his lips from hers and caressed her cheek. "You know how much I love you."

Hearing the words still made her warm all over.

No matter what she did or said, he loved her, and the power of that love left her in awe. "I know."

"If you ever need a break, want to explore other options since you never had a chance to before—"

She rose on the balls of her feet and silenced him with a kiss. Before she'd become involved with him, she hadn't relied on anyone. Had never truly trusted anyone. To have another person love her, body and soul, was a remarkable thing that she didn't take for granted.

For the first time in forever, she was filled with optimism for the future. For a future with him. "I keep telling you—I want *you*," she said. "I love you. In fact, I was thinking that maybe in the spring, I'd put my house up for sale. We're together all the time anyway." Aside from work, they were inseparable.

"Okay."

She smiled. "That's all? Okay?" No hesitation?

"Yeah. You're the person I need to hold on to. I just didn't want to hold on too tightly."

"Hold on as tightly as you want. I'm not fragile. I won't break. Just don't let go."

"The brave, strong woman I know is anything but fragile." He placed a tender kiss on her lips. "And I'll never let go." His smile was soft and only for her.

Life was beautiful. Nora looked around at all the beaming faces, absorbing the joy that overflowed in the room. She'd not only found friends and family in these fearless people who fought for her, but she'd also found something in Bitterroot Falls that she'd been too scared to think possible. Love and a home—where she was going to build a life with Bo.

* * * * *

Get up to 4 Free Books!

**We'll send you 2 free books from each series you try
PLUS a free Mystery Gift.**

FREE Value Over **$25**

Both the **Harlequin Intrigue®** and **Harlequin® Romantic Suspense** series feature compelling novels filled with heart-racing action-packed romance that will keep you on the edge of your seat.

YES! Please send me 2 FREE novels from the Harlequin Intrigue or Harlequin Romantic Suspense series and my FREE gift (gift is worth about $10 retail). After receiving them, if I don't wish to receive any more books, I can return the shipping statement marked "cancel." If I don't cancel, I will receive 6 brand-new Harlequin Intrigue Larger-Print books every month and be billed just $7.19 each in the U.S. or $7.99 each in Canada, or 4 brand-new Harlequin Romantic Suspense books every month and be billed just $6.39 each in the U.S. or $7.19 each in Canada, a savings of 20% off the cover price. It's quite a bargain! Shipping and handling is just 50¢ per book in the U.S. and $1.25 per book in Canada.* I understand that accepting the 2 free books and gift places me under no obligation to buy anything. I can always return a shipment and cancel at any time by calling the number below. The free books and gift are mine to keep no matter what I decide.

Choose one:
- ☐ **Harlequin Intrigue Larger-Print** (199/399 BPA G36Y)
- ☐ **Harlequin Romantic Suspense** (240/340 BPA G36Y)
- ☐ **Or Try Both!** (199/399 & 240/340 BPA G36Z)

Name (please print)

Address   Apt. #

City   State/Province   Zip/Postal Code

Email: Please check this box ☐ if you would like to receive newsletters and promotional emails from Harlequin Enterprises ULC and its affiliates. You can unsubscribe anytime.

Mail to the Harlequin Reader Service:
IN U.S.A.: P.O. Box 1341, Buffalo, NY 14240-8531
IN CANADA: P.O. Box 603, Fort Erie, Ontario L2A 5X3

Want to explore our other series or interested in ebooks? **Visit www.ReaderService.com or call 1-800-873-8635.**

---

*Terms and prices subject to change without notice. Prices do not include sales taxes, which will be charged (if applicable) based on your state or country of residence. Canadian residents will be charged applicable taxes. Offer not valid in Quebec. This offer is limited to one order per household. Books received may not be as shown. Not valid for current subscribers to the Harlequin Intrigue or Harlequin Romantic Suspense series. All orders subject to approval. Credit or debit balances in a customer's account(s) may be offset by any outstanding balance owed by or to the customer. Please allow 4 to 6 weeks for delivery. Offer available while quantities last.

Your Privacy—Your information is being collected by Harlequin Enterprises ULC, operating as Harlequin Reader Service. For a complete summary of the information we collect, how we use this information and to whom it is disclosed, please visit our privacy notice located at https://corporate.harlequin.com/privacy-notice. Notice to California Residents – Under California law, you have specific rights to control and access your data. For more information on these rights and how to exercise them, visit https://corporate.harlequin.com/california-privacy. For additional information for residents of other U.S. states that provide their residents with certain rights with respect to personal data, visit https://corporate.harlequin.com/other-state-residents-privacy-rights/.

HIHRS25